OLD FLAME

OLD FLAME

•

Liz Thompson

AVALON BOOKS
NEW YORK

To my parents, who taught me to dream,
to my husband and children, who give me the love and
freedom to chase that dream,
and to Erin Cartwright, who helped me fulfill my dream.
Thank you for everything.

Chapter One

The sweet-faced toddler opened her cherry-pink mouth and let out a screech of such magnitude that had Courtney not been her daughter, Annie Palmer Wylie would have sworn the child had suffered a heinous injury, a broken limb, a nasty contusion—something. Instead, an even worse fate had befallen little Courtney. At the tender age of twenty-three months, two weeks, and four days, she had once again been told "no, no" in a stern voice.

"That will teach me," Annie muttered as her daughter fell to the floor and followed the screech with her entire tantrum repertoire—the half-sob with a partial hiccup on the end, the racking wail with the pudgy fingers across the face, and finally, the heartfelt boo-hoo with the trembling lip thrown in for good measure.

It was, by even Courtney's high standards, an outstanding tantrum performance.

Realizing that Courtney had drawn a crowd at the only grocery store in Summerly, New Hampshire, Annie squatted next to her daughter and tried reasoning. "Pea Pod, Mommy's not mad. It's just that Mommy doesn't want you to eat a candy bar now."

Courtney continued her tantrum. Even though her vocabulary at the moment consisted of only about a dozen words, she understood enough to realize that Mommy's words might sound pretty, but they still meant *no.*

"Okay, honey, let's do it this way." Annie slid her arms under the tiny body and tried to lift. It resembled one of those clown acts in the circus where the big clown can't lift the little clown. Courtney, weighing in at just under twenty-eight pounds, stiffened her torso in such a manner that it was almost impossible for Annie to get a solid grip on her. It was like trying to hold a thrashing board. Every time Annie thought she had the girl, Courtney slung her body the opposite way, causing Annie to almost lose her grip. Fearing she would drop her daughter, Annie relaxed her hold and tried again.

After a few minutes, Annie groaned in frustration. Courtney wasn't giving up her fight. With one final lunge, Annie grabbed her daughter and tried to stand. She would have made it too, if Courtney hadn't come out of nowhere with a left hook any prizefighter would envy. The punch connected with a thud to Annie's nose. Annie teetered for a moment, and then felt her high heels give way from under her.

"Oh, no."

Twisting her body with unconscious maternal instinct, Annie landed flat on her back with Courtney cushioned against her chest. The drop was so fast and so hard that it momentarily knocked the wind out of Annie. The crowd that had been watching the scene moved forward, leaning as a group over her prone body. Annie closed her eyes for a second, not wanting to see the collection of faces—some amused, others concerned, and a few latecomers, perplexed.

"I think that's a TKO."

Wait a minute: that voice. She knew that man's voice. For years she'd heard it in her head, the timbre sliding over her nerves like warm summer rain. It was Tyler Nelson.

"Are you okay?" he asked.

She shook her head, but not in answer to his question. *Oh, no. Please, no. Not him. I'll be good. I promise. I won't ever scold Courtney again. I'll donate more to charity. Okay, I'll even eat broccoli. Just don't let it be Tyler.*

"Are you just going to lie there all night? I'm used to women falling at my feet, but this is a bit much," he said.

So much for bargaining, Annie thought. She tipped her head back and looked into the same wicked green eyes that she still occasionally saw in a dream. Twelve years unwound in a heartbeat, and she was again dating the most popular boy in town.

"What are you doing here?" she asked, still hoping that the blow to her head had caused her to see things.

Then he grinned, and she knew he was real. No one man on the planet but Tyler Nelson had that butter-melting grin. At the moment, he hunkered behind her head, surveying her condition. He looked the same as he had the last time she'd seen him. To tell the truth, he looked even better. His brown hair still fell across his forehead; his forest green eyes still sparkled with that tempting gleam. Even the presence of a few laugh lines on his face didn't detract from his good looks. If anything, they enhanced the overall effect of his handsome face.

Then there was the grin. Even after all these years, Annie remembered how it worked wonders on women—all women—girlfriends, teachers, waitresses . . . That grin never failed. And judging from the smile on her daughter's face, it worked on the preverbal age group, too.

"Hello, Annie," Tyler said.

Two large hands reached out and took Courtney off her chest. Rather than protesting, Courtney seemed delighted with the prospect. She went willingly into the arms of the one man Annie had wanted to avoid for the rest of her life. It had been her birthday wish every year since she'd moved back to town. Right before she blew out the candles, she would close her eyes, wish for health and happiness for her family, and then hope that she never had to see Tyler Nelson again. Apparently wishing didn't work any better than bargaining did.

Tyler tucked Courtney against his chest, holding her steady with one strong arm. He extended his free hand to Annie.

"Can I help you?"

Annie ignored his hand and sat up. With as much grace as she could muster, she put her palms flat on the floor and shoved herself to her feet. Tyler rose with her.

Well, at least the crowd had dispersed. She brushed off the skirt of her gray-and-white print dress, avoiding direct eye contact with Tyler. Wasn't that what you did with most wild animals? she thought. Avoid direct eye contact, and they may leave you alone.

She reached out her hands. "Please give me my daughter."

Tyler laughed. "That's it? After all these years, the only thing you have to say to me is 'give me my daughter'—no hello, how are you, nice to see you?"

Annie dragged in a deep breath. This shouldn't be happening. It wasn't supposed to happen. The one time she'd finally worked up her nerve to ask about him, her mother had assured her that he rarely came to town. He was too busy and successful to come back to Summerly, which was good, of course. Annie had been relieved to know there was no chance of running into Tyler.

So why was he standing here in front of her, holding her daughter, looking too handsome for her own peace of mind? Like Dorian Gray, whatever sins he'd committed so far in life weren't showing on his face. It was a masculine masterpiece, and she silently cursed herself for still feeling attracted to him. Wasn't there a statute of limitations on attraction?

She wasn't in the mood for this today. With an effort, Annie forced the muscles in her face to form a tight smile. It was weak and unnatural, but it would have to do.

"Hello, Tyler. How are you? It's nice to see you. Sorry, but I have to go." She was being rude, and she knew it. It nudged against her conscience, but it was the best she could do. Even after all this time, it was impossible for her to stand there and make small talk with this man.

She leaned forward and tried to take Courtney from his arms, but he took a step back and swung the toddler onto his hip.

"Come on, Annie. Give me a break. Here I am, thrilled and excited to see you, and you're about as welcoming as a porcupine. You can't possibly be mad after all these years."

Was she *mad?* Annie wondered. Of course she wasn't. Why should she be? She'd adored him, heck, almost worshiped him. Then he'd dropped her the week before their wedding because she didn't have impressive bloodlines. Her parents hadn't been part of the same country club crowd as Tyler's parents were. They didn't play golf and go to the theater together. No, her parents owned an auto repair shop.

Their breakup had become a joke around town. People had teased her dad because his daughter wasn't good enough for the Nelson boy. Her father was a proud man, and Annie knew the taunts had eaten at him for quite some time.

But that was in the past, right? She wasn't eighteen anymore, and her crush on Tyler was history. It had been a life lesson, like when Courtney learned not to put beans up her nose. As was true with most lessons, it had been painful, but when it was over, one had learned something.

Annie rubbed her hands along the sides of her skirt, suddenly noticing a large black stain. "No, I'm not mad. I'm just very busy."

Rather than being upset, Tyler smiled, his green eyes twinkling, his killer dimple appearing. "You are *too* still mad. You can't fool me. How about if I admit up front that I was stupid? I should have handled things . . . differently. But we were both way too young to get married, so it all worked out in the end, right?" He bounced Courtney on his hip, making her giggle.

Annie sighed. He was over thirty and still pouring

on the charm. "Really, I've got to go. Please give me my daughter."

Tyler looked down into Courtney's smiling face and then back at Annie. His grin never dimmed, but the twinkle in his eyes disappeared as he studied her. She could tell he was sizing her up, and she didn't like it one bit. She knew what he saw when he looked at her. She'd aged and changed and was different in a million ways from the lovesick teenager who had thrown herself at the town's favorite son. She wore her black hair short now because she was too busy to fuss with it, and her hazel eyes showed the fatigue that overwhelmed her by this time of day. But probably the only thing Tyler would notice was how her figure had rounded since Courtney's birth.

She didn't say anything. Instead, she just lifted her chin and defied him to comment on the changes. She wouldn't let him know how self-conscious she felt. It had been a long day, and she knew she looked rumpled. But it no longer concerned her how she looked to Tyler Nelson.

When he'd finished his survey, he said, "Your daughter's cute. And you've grown into a beautiful woman." He tapped the end of Courtney's pug nose and received a tooth-scattered smile in return. "What did you do to this princess to send her into such a tizzy?"

Annie sighed. This run-in with Tyler really was too much. First the crazy day at the store, then the trouble with the computer, and now this. All she wanted was to go home, take an aspirin, and give Courtney her bath. "I didn't do anything. She's almost two, and she's prone to tantrums."

Courtney had such an angelic expression on her face at the moment, it was difficult to believe she'd ever misbehaved in her life. She lifted her plump fingers and tugged on a strand of Tyler's dark brown hair, which lay against the collar of his shirt.

"I don't believe it," Tyler teased. "This perfect child would never behave like that unless provoked."

Annie opened her mouth to protest, and then slammed it shut. No, she wasn't going to do this. She wasn't a kid anymore. She no longer played these sorts of games. For years, she'd worked at one of the biggest computer companies in Boston. During that time, she'd learned a lot of useful information, not the least of which was to hold firm to one's ground, and never blink first.

She smiled. "It really was nice to see you again, Tyler, but I'm busy right now, so unless you plan on kidnapping my daughter, I suggest you give her back." Her tone was forthright and firm. She got more than a little satisfaction out of watching a surprised look cross his face. Now he knew she wasn't a pushover anymore.

He rubbed his hand across his chin, apparently debating his next move. She watched him warily, and when a gleam appeared in his eyes, she braced herself.

"Now, sweetheart, is that any way to talk to your first love? Seems to me you should be a little more friendly."

It was such an outrageous thing to say that she didn't know whether to be insulted or amused.

"You were *not* my first love. I was in love at least twice before I met you." She almost regretted her words when he looked genuinely offended by what she'd said.

"I don't think I believe you." He gave her his trademark smoldering look. Even after all these years, after marriage and a child, that look made the blood flood to her face.

The old joke from high school came back to her. Know what caused global warming? Tyler Nelson smiled at a group of women.

"Been here, done this." She walked over and put her hands on her grocery cart. "Since you won't return Courtney, I guess I should tell you she's a really good eater. If it's smaller than she is and slows down, she'll eat it. But her favorite food is spaghetti, her bedtime is at seven, and she loves to watch Barney tapes." Without a backward look, she started down the aisle.

"Where's your husband?"

She wasn't surprised to see that Tyler had fallen into step next to her. His tone sounded neutral, and she forced herself to keep her own that way, too. "Dead."

Tyler stopped in the middle of the aisle. Annie turned and looked back over her shoulder at him, waiting for him to recover and catch up. The compassionate look on his face made her regret dropping the news on him like that. Even though seeing Tyler after all this time had thrown her, it really didn't justify being so mean. She counted to ten, then to twenty. She needed to try harder to be nice.

"I'm sorry." Tyler walked slowly toward her. "Mother never told me. She said you'd moved back to town, but she didn't tell me you'd been married nor mention the baby."

That was no surprise to Annie. Marguerite Nelson hadn't been fond of her, so why would she share any information about her with Tyler?

"No, I'm sorry, Tyler. I shouldn't have said it like that." She ran her hand through her short hair, fluffing the tendrils near her face. "I've had a long day."

He nodded. "I understand. I feel bad bringing it up. When I saw you just now, I assumed your husband was at home or at work." He put one large hand on her shoulder. "I really am sorry."

Annie didn't look at him. She kept her gaze straight ahead. It was difficult for her to talk about Paul. He was still very much a part of her life—his smile, his eyes—she saw them whenever she looked at her daughter, a daughter he'd never seen, never even known was on the way. "Thanks. So am I."

She'd missed cereal, so she had to back up and retrace her steps. "How did it happen?"

"Car accident." She drew in a shallow breath, feeling the familiar tightness in her chest. The last thing she wanted to do was stand here discussing Paul with Tyler. "Look, can we please not go into this?"

Tyler studied her carefully. After a moment, his ever-present smile returned, but his eyes were still full of compassion. "Sure."

"Good."

Annie went up and down two more aisles with Tyler trailing next to her before the silence between them drove her crazy. Just being this close to him made the nerves in her body hum with awareness. Finally, she spun toward him. "Why don't you tell me how exciting your life has become."

Courtney was trying to poke him in the eye, so he shifted her to his other hip, distracting her. "I'm a lawyer."

"So I heard." Actually, she'd more than heard it. She'd read about several of his cases in the paper. Not surprisingly, Tyler's flash and flare served him well on important cases. That razzle-dazzle charm probably had juries eating out of his hand.

"I don't enjoy it much anymore," he said. Before he could add anything else, Courtney leaned forward and tried to bite his cheek. Tyler jerked his head back and held Courtney away from him. "I see she takes after you—she screams and bites."

Annie told herself not to laugh, but she couldn't help it. "I trained her well." She reached out, and this time, Tyler turned over the child. Annie had expected another tantrum when she tried to put Courtney in the buggy seat, but instead, the little girl went willingly. Taking advantage of the momentary bout of cooperation, Annie quickly fastened the belt around the toddler's waist.

Tyler nodded toward the thin black seat belt. "Will that keep her in?"

"As long as she lets it. She knows how to unfasten the belt, but when she's in a good mood, she tolerates it."

"I see."

Courtney smiled at Tyler, and Annie had to resist the temptation to tell her daughter not to fall for him. But Tyler was too much for the little girl to resist. He leaned down and dropped several light, smacking kisses on her temple. Courtney giggled and beamed at him.

"Man. Man," Courtney said.

"Hey, she's pretty smart." Tyler gave Courtney another kiss.

Annie shook her head. "Sorry to disappoint you. To Courtney, everything's a man—men, women, cats, dogs, trees—everything."

"Oh. So how do you know what she's talking about?"

"I guess." Annie pushed her cart in line, surprised to see she'd actually been able to do her shopping with Tyler along. Not only had she done it, but because

Courtney had behaved, it hadn't been the ordeal it usually was.

"And the tantrums?" he asked. "Is that what happens when you guess wrong?"

"Yes. Or if I say no."

He seemed to consider that for a while, then he turned and smiled at her. Rather than his usual crooked grin, this smile was sincere.

"So, when am I coming to your house for dinner?" he asked. Amazed, Annie stared at him. He couldn't seriously think they'd pick up where they'd left off. The man had jilted her. Sure, his family had picked up the tab on any outstanding bills for the wedding, but money couldn't make up for shredded feelings.

Beyond that, Annie didn't want Tyler back in her life. She needed to keep herself focused on her family's business. Her father and brother were talking about expanding to stay competitive with the big companies moving into town. But money was much too tight to do something risky, such as expanding.

"Sorry, Tyler," she said, "but you're not coming over to my house. We've had a nice reunion, but this is it. Now go visit your mother and then fly off to wherever it is you live." Deliberately, Annie turned away from him and tipped her head, so she could read the headlines on the tabloids. Her nerves couldn't stand any more. As much as she liked to pretend seeing him hadn't thrown her system into shock, she couldn't. Tyler had really hurt her when he'd called

off the wedding, and she'd taken all the casual conversation she could stand.

Rather than take her hint, Tyler shifted until he
blocked her view.

"You're not making this easy," he said. "I'm trying
my hardest to sweep you off your feet."

"News flash—it isn't working." She shifted to the
side, picked up a magazine, and pretended to read the
cover. "I'm not even close to being swept off my feet."

He grinned. "Really? So why are you reading that?"

"What?"

He nodded toward the magazine.

Annie glanced down and then groaned. Plastered
across the front of the magazine in giant type was the
headline: Twenty Guaranteed Ways to Make Him Fall
in Love. She knew Tyler was just waiting for her to
blush, so instead, she flipped open the magazine and
skimmed through the pages. "Just because you didn't
manage to sweep me off my feet doesn't mean someone else can't."

He laughed loud enough to draw the attention of the
people in the next aisle. His deep green eyes were
shining as he looked at her. "I guess I deserve that."

"Yes, you do. Now why don't you go back to where
you came from?"

"I came from here."

"You know what I mean."

"Wow, you sure are prickly," he said. "Sorry to disappoint you, but I'm not leaving for a while. Mom

hasn't been well, so I'm going to stick around for a few weeks."

Annie thought hard. She was almost through this, and if she played her cards right, she would never have to see Tyler again. "I'm sorry to hear about your mother. Rather than going out to dinner, you should stay close to home then, in case she needs you."

Tyler ran one hand through his hair, ruffling it. It should have looked messy, but instead, it looked even nicer as it fell across his forehead. "Yeah, you're probably right."

She resisted the self-congratulating smile that longed to form on her lips. "So, we'll say good-bye now."

"No, I'll just bring Mom with me. I know she'd love to see you."

The thought of Marguerite Nelson in her house almost made Annie laugh. She doubted Tyler's mother would ever consider setting one pristine foot in the lowly house of Annie Palmer Wylie.

"Tyler, stop this. I'm not having you over for dinner."

He blinked at her. "I didn't say you were. I wasn't talking to you."

"What?"

He bent over the tousled blond head in the cart. "Your mama is so stuck on herself, she actually believed we were coming to visit *her.*" He kissed Courtney's forehead. "See you Wednesday night at six."

Walking away, he pretended he couldn't hear Annie calling after him.

"I won't be there. I'll stand you up, Tyler Nelson." She looked around. The people in the surrounding lines stared at her. Several of them she knew, and since they knew her past history with Tyler, it made this spectacle all the more embarrassing. She smiled sheepishly and started unloading her cart on the revolving counter.

"Men. They will torment you your entire life, Courtney. Watch out for them, Pea Pod, and whatever you do, don't take them too seriously."

Courtney smiled up at her mother, her dimples on full display, melting Annie's heart.

"Man. Man."

Tyler couldn't remember a time when he'd been so pleased with himself. Walking across the parking lot to his car, he grinned. Annie had looked great. From the second he'd come back into town, he'd wondered about her. For years he'd felt like a heel because of the way their engagement had ended. He knew what everyone had said about him, and he'd grown up enough in the last few years to realize what a low-down lizard he'd been to let his father push him away from Annie.

But at the time, his old man had been Tyler's world, and pleasing him had meant everything. Shortly after he'd entered college, he'd realized his father didn't know everything. It had been a tough time, and the two of them had fought constantly. Finally, like all children, Tyler had realized that nowhere was it written that his father was the only perfect person on the planet. After that, they'd finally settled into a relationship where they supported each other's good points and ignored the bad ones as much as possible.

However, Henry Nelson had died. Even after all these years, Tyler still missed him.

He climbed into his Porsche and started the engine, but he didn't put the car into drive. Instead, he stared across the parking lot at the door to the grocery store. Annie came out carrying Courtney on her hip. A teenaged boy pushed her cart, and it looked as if Courtney had launched into another tantrum. It was weird thinking of Annie as a mom. Heck, it was weird thinking of Annie as married. Until tonight, Annie had been frozen in his mind at eighteen, pretty and happy. He was in trouble.

Tyler sighed and put his car in drive. Well, Annie was wrong about one thing. His mother would be thrilled to know he'd bumped into her. Years ago, Marguerite had also mistakenly thought Annie wasn't good enough for her son, But as time passed, and he showed less and less inclination toward marriage and giving her grandchildren, his mother had become receptive to all candidates.

Unfortunately, his mother was bound to be disappointed again. Now was the least likely time for him to think about marriage. He hadn't a clue about what he intended to do with the rest of his life, let alone with whom he expected to spend it. His mother's illness had made him rethink a lot of things, not the least of which was whether he really wanted to continue living in New York. More and more, he was considering coming back to Summerly for an extended stay.

Summerly was especially attractive to him now that Annie's brother, Kevin, had called with a partnership idea. Staying for a prolonged period of time in Summerly was a possibility, but still, that would mean walking away from the law firm. He wasn't sure he could do that, not just yet anyway.

Tyler pulled his car up to the electronic gate in front of his mother's house and pressed the button. After the scrolled metal gates swung open, he drove his car around the circular drive and headed toward the garage in back. Even though only his mother lived here now, the house and the grounds were maintained flawlessly.

He parked and walked in through the kitchen, where he found his mother sitting at the breakfast table talking to the housekeeper. Dolores had worked for the family for twenty years, and Tyler suspected she was less of an employee to his mother now and more of a friend. When he came home he usually found the two of them talking.

"Hey, gorgeous." He brushed a kiss on his mother's forehead and dropped into the chair next to her.

"Did you get the apples?" Dolores asked.

He knew he'd forgotten something. He'd been so excited to see Annie that he'd completely forgotten why he'd gone to the grocery store in the first place.

"Sorry. I got distracted."

Marguerite raised one eyebrow. "Distracted by whom?"

He grinned. "Annie Palmer. She was there with her daughter."

His mother's expression brightened. "Her last name is Wylie now. How is she?"

Tyler inwardly debated how to handle this. He knew his mother felt guilty about what had happened with Annie years ago. She'd been too quick to judge the young woman, and it wasn't easy for someone reared the way Marguerite had been to admit that she was wrong. But time and life had mellowed his mother and taught her that many of the arbitrary standards she'd held were flat-out wrong. Certain people weren't better than others simply because their bank accounts contained more zeros.

Marguerite's friendship with Dolores was an example. For years, his mother had maintained a firm distance from her housekeeper. But after Tyler had moved out, and his father had passed away, Dolores had been kind to his mother. That kindness had grown into a friendship based on mutual respect, rather than on who paid whom.

"Annie looks great," Tyler said. "And her daughter is a real sweetheart."

Marguerite nodded. "She's cute. Fran babysits her granddaughter sometimes. I've run into them at the mall."

So his mother was at least speaking to Fran Palmer. Well, that was progress of some sort. If Annie's mom didn't hold a grudge, then maybe Annie wouldn't get upset when she found out what he and Kevin had planned.

"Did either of you ever meet Annie's husband?" Tyler asked.

Both his mother and Dolores shook their heads. "Annie moved back to town after he was killed," Dolores said. "The baby was born here."

That meant Annie's husband had been dead for some time. Tyler hadn't wanted to ask in the grocery store, but he'd been curious. Annie had said Courtney was around two.

"Have you talked to Annie lately?" he asked.

He looked at his mother, but she just shrugged. "I . . . um . . . haven't spoken to Annie since . . ."

Her voice trailed off and an embarrassed silence fell over the kitchen. Yes, his mother hadn't spoken to Annie since he'd dumped her. There wasn't much in his life that he was truly ashamed of. He'd made mistakes, but they'd been honest errors. Dropping Annie was his low moment. He'd truly believed he was in love with her, but still he'd let his parents convince him that marriage would ruin both of their lives. Now, in retrospect, he suspected that his parents had thought Annie wasn't good enough for him.

But in truth, she'd been *too* good for him. Annie wouldn't have let anyone put him down. She wouldn't have let appearances stop her from seeing him. He'd run with a fast crowd that got away with too much because their parents had money. With his wild reputation around town, no doubt her parents hadn't been thrilled when she'd started dating him. Annie's father had glared at him every time he'd shown up to take her out.

But still Annie had gone out with him. She hadn't let others tell her what to do.

Tyler sighed. Maybe it was too late to do anything about this. Maybe he was being silly for even trying. Twelve years was a long time, and neither of them were kids anymore. There was no way to go back and make up for the past.

He glanced at his mother. She looked tired, and he knew this conversation was upsetting to her. He leaned across the table and kissed her cheek. "Don't fret. It isn't good for you."

Marguerite patted his hand. "Did Annie seem happy to see you? Or was she angry? Fran's always nice to me, but I'm not sure if Annie's father and brother are still mad. You know how they feel about you."

Well, he'd thought he did, until Kevin Palmer had called him last week. Tyler had never expected to hear from Kevin again. Annie's brother had threatened him with a wrench the Monday after he'd broken up with Annie.

"People change over time," Tyler said, not wanting to explain his plans with Kevin to his mother until everything was finalized. He'd promised Kevin he wouldn't tell anyone, and he wouldn't break that promise.

Marguerite looked doubtful. "Some people don't."

He shrugged. Kevin had changed. And Tyler knew he had too. Years ago, he would never have agreed to help fund expansion on the Palmer family auto repair store. But now the idea held infinite appeal to him, especially since he'd seen Annie.

Realizing his mother and Dolores were staring at him, he said, "Mom, I'm not interested in Annie. But her daughter and I have a date to have spaghetti on Wednesday, and you're invited. Courtney and I became friends today."

Both Dolores and his mother laughed, so he quit while he was ahead. He'd just gotten home, and he had a lot of things to sort out. He would like to smooth things over with Annie and her family. Hopefully, giving them much-needed capital would help. Tyler also owed the entire Palmer family an apology. But that was it; he'd never get involved with Annie again because one thing hadn't changed over the years—Annie had been a forever-type girl—and now she was a forever-type woman.

And he'd never been a forever-type man.

Chapter Two

She'd thought he'd been kidding. How could he *not* have been kidding? Even Tyler Nelson, with his giant-sized ego, had to know a brush-off when one hit him smack between the eyes. At least, she'd hoped so. So when her doorbell rang on Wednesday night, she didn't give it a thought. She padded over to get it wearing her frayed jeans and faded T-shirt.

Tyler stood on her front porch with a bottle of wine in one hand and a bottle of apple juice in the other. Even more surprising was that his mother stood next to him. Marguerite Nelson smiled at Annie as if they'd been friends for years.

"Where's Courtney?" Tyler asked before Annie could say anything.

Annie returned Marguerite's smile and then turned to Tyler. "What are you doing here?"

Without waiting to be invited, he nudged past her into the living room. "I'm here to have dinner with Courtney." He glanced around the room. "I see your mom and dad haven't arrived yet."

"Why would they be here? I didn't invite them." Annoyed, she followed Tyler into the living room.

Tyler grinned. *"I* did. I thought we all could catch up on old times."

Annie felt like a pressure cooker about to explode. How dare he take over her life like this? "Is anyone else coming?" she asked, her voice dripping with sarcasm.

"Kevin." Tyler shrugged. "I don't know if he's bringing a date."

Marguerite had tentatively followed her son inside the house. "Is there a problem?"

At the hesitation in the other woman's voice, Annie turned and looked at her. She saw a woman who'd changed over the years. Gone was the regal attitude Marguerite used to have. In its place was a milder, more considerate demeanor. Twice in recent months, Marguerite had brought her car into the shop for repairs. Annie hadn't had a chance to talk to her, but from what she'd seen, Marguerite had been nice to everyone. Maybe people really could change, or maybe time had just mellowed Marguerite Nelson.

At the moment, Marguerite looked so sad that Annie couldn't stop herself from saying, "No, there's no problem. Of course you're welcome." She shot Tyler a blazing look and then turned back to Marguerite. "I just needed to know who was coming."

Tyler's smug grin almost made Annie retract her words, but before she had a chance to tell him what she thought of him, Courtney padded into the room. She took one look at Tyler and toddled over to him, her arms up in the air.

"Man. Man."

Tyler picked her up and gave her a hug. "Hey there, gorgeous." Courtney rewarded him with a sloppy kiss. He turned to his mother. "Have you met Courtney yet?"

Marguerite came over and patted Courtney's arm, a wide smile on her face. "What a beautiful child." She glanced at Annie. "You're so lucky to have her."

Annie nodded, wondering at what point she'd lost control of her life. It had happened in the grocery store. Up until that point, she'd been fine. But the second she'd stepped through those automatic doors, she must have crossed into "The Twilight Zone."

Tyler put Courtney on his hip and grinned at Annie. "Since I'm responsible for this party, I took the liberty of bringing food."

He turned and walked out the front door before Annie could say a word. After he'd disappeared, Marguerite smiled at her. "I hope you don't mind.

Tyler didn't want you to go to any trouble, so he made the sauce at home. He's a very good cook."

Annie nodded. He sure was. He'd cooked up this doozie of a scheme. What she couldn't understand, though, was why he'd done it. It didn't make sense. It wasn't as if he wanted a date. He'd not only brought along his own mother, he'd also invited her entire family. What on earth was he up to?

When Tyler and Courtney returned from getting the food from his car, Annie was ready to ask him a few well-chosen questions, but her family arrived at that moment. Her mother, father, and brother, Kevin, laughed and joked with Tyler as if he were some prodigal son who'd finally returned home.

During the next few minutes, Annie decided they were all up to something. It wasn't just Tyler, her family didn't act like this. Sure they laughed and joked, but they didn't smile such inane smiles.

And everyone was constantly smiling at one another. It drove Annie nuts. For starters, her father and brother had vowed years ago to have nothing further to do with the Nelson family. Yet here they both were, stirring spaghetti with Tyler in her kitchen. Meanwhile, at her tiny kitchen table, her mother and Marguerite chattered like two teenagers who'd been best friends for years. Annie wanted to grab them, shake them, and demand that they tell her where they'd hidden her real family.

In the middle of it all was Courtney. One person

after another scooped her up and gave her hugs and kisses. Little Courtney was in her element—being adored by a room full of grown-ups who intended to feed her spaghetti. For a two-year-old life couldn't get any better.

When the laughter in the kitchen got too loud, Annie went out to the living room and flopped down in her favorite chair. It wasn't like anyone would miss her in her own house. They had invaded, and she was no longer needed.

"Want to talk about it?"

She tipped her head back and glanced at Tyler. "Why are you doing this to me?"

He came to the side of her chair and crouched so that he was eye-level with her. Gently, he brushed a loose strand of hair from her cheek. "I'm not doing anything to you, Annie."

His soft voice ran over her like warm water. "Yes, you are. You're up to something."

He hesitated for a second, then shook his head slowly; the expression in his eyes was one of sadness. And there was something else, some indefinable emotion she didn't recognize. "I haven't seen your folks in years. It seemed like a nice idea to ask them to come."

No wonder this man was a terror in the courtroom. He had such a convincing voice, it was easy to believe everything he said. Of course, that was until you got to know what a louse he could be. And Annie knew it didn't take much to make that sincere tone of his change.

"I don't believe a word you say," Annie admitted. "I wish I never had."

Tyler frowned. "I know. I can't tell you how sorry I am about the past."

Annie sat up straight in her chair. Talking about the past was difficult for her at the best of times. It was almost impossible with Tyler so close to her, looking so handsome. Still, he was making an effort, so she would too. "Apology accepted. But to be honest, I don't want you in my house."

Instead of being insulted, Tyler chuckled. "At least you let me have it straight. Still, this will make it difficult for me to see Courtney."

Annie blinked at him. Was he really crazy? "I don't want you to see Courtney."

"But Courtney wants to see me."

"Courtney's two. She doesn't know what she wants."

Tyler shook his head slowly and made an annoying tsking sound. "Now you know that's not true. She likes me."

"She'll get over it," Annie said slowly. "I don't want you coming over here again."

Tyler tipped his head and studied her as if she were a piece of unexpected evidence brought into the court-room. It gave Annie a certain degree of satisfaction to watch comprehension slowly dawn on his handsome face. It had taken him some time, but she was relatively certain he now knew she was serious.

"Fine. But can we at least have dinner tonight?" Tyler asked.

Thank goodness he'd finally gotten the hint. Annie smiled her first true smile since Tyler had appeared on her doorstep. "Okay, dinner tonight. But that's it. No more sneakiness."

"Well, I wasn't exactly sneaky. I told you in the grocery store I'd be over for dinner tonight."

"And I told you not to come," Annie pointed out.

"You should have had Courtney tell me. She's the one who asked me over."

He gave her that trademark crooked grin again. There really was no dealing with the man. Annie sighed. What was the point? He truly was insane. "Fine. Well, from now on, when Courtney asks you over, tell her you're busy."

"I don't like to lie."

"Of course you do. You've always been very good at it. That's why you're such a good lawyer—you can say anything and make other people believe it's true."

Tyler gazed at her for a moment, his green eyes twinkling with humor. "Now what did you do for fun all those years when you didn't have me around to criticize?"

"I made do."

A loud noise from the kitchen caused Tyler to turn his head for a moment. At this close range, it was difficult for Annie to ignore how good-looking he was. That was the unfair part—nobody as sneaky as he was should possess so much appeal. It just wasn't right.

When Tyler turned his head back toward her, he winked. "I think I'd better hurry before we're interrupted."

Annie frowned, not liking that statement one bit. "What do you mean?"

Tyler's expression reminded her of the look that crossed Courtney's face whenever the toddler had something bad planned. Annie shifted back in the chair, trying to gain some distance from him. But her move didn't help; Tyler leaned forward and put one hand on either chair arm, effectively blocking her in.

"Tyler, back off," she said.

He tipped his head and considered her. "The way I see it, you're already so mad at me, you'd like to scream. I figure I can't hurt things by doing this."

She opened her mouth to ask what *this* was, but before the words escaped her, Tyler swooped in and kissed her. His action surprised Annie so much, it took a moment for her to realize what was happening. Then, just as she was about to push him away, the warmth of his kiss held her in place. Tyler had always been a great kisser, and the years had just improved on perfection.

Tyler's hands moved from the chair arms and rested lightly on either side of her waist. He did nothing to trap her, but she felt that way all the same. It had been far too long since she'd been kissed. Without really intending to, she raised her hand and placed it along the side of his face. For one short moment, life was as it used to be. She was young and in love and—

The cry from the kitchen made her jerk her head back. She stared at Tyler for a breathless second, then she pushed him away and headed toward the kitchen to see what was wrong with Courtney. She found her daughter sitting on Marguerite's lap, big tears running down her small face.

Annie could only hope she didn't look as guilty as she felt. Her face was warm, and she prayed she wasn't blushing. The last thing she wanted was for the people in this room to suspect what had just happened.

"What's wrong?" Annie asked, keeping her voice as steady as possible. Thankfully, Tyler hadn't followed her, so she had a few minutes to restore her shaky composure.

"Nothing. Courtney wanted to go near the hot stove, and we wouldn't let her," her mother said.

"Oh." Annie shifted her balance from one leg to the other. Now that she was in the crowded kitchen with everyone else, she felt self-conscious. What was wrong with her? She was as crazy as the rest of them. She never should have let Tyler kiss her.

"Where's Tyler?"

Annie blinked at her father. "Tyler?"

He laughed and dropped his arm around her shoulders. "He went to find you."

Oh, he'd found her all right. "He's in the living room." Everyone in the kitchen was looking at her with expressions varying from mild interest to down-right skepticism. "He and I were talking," she said lamely.

Herb Palmer grinned. "Okay. If that's what you say."

Annie moved away from her father and avoided looking at him. "That's what we were doing." She bent and scooped Courtney off Marguerite's lap, thankful for the distraction the child offered.

"I need to change her before dinner," she said as she left the kitchen and entered the living room.

She was about to release a pent-up sigh when she ran smack into Tyler. He reached out and caught her with his hands, steadying her. Since Annie held Courtney in her arms, she was trapped.

Annie stared up at him. "Don't take this the wrong way, Tyler, but buzz off."

He laughed and kissed Courtney's upturned face. "Hey there, sweetheart."

Courtney giggled. "Man. Man."

"See, she does too know who I am." Tapping the toddler on the nose, he said, "Your mama's really mad at me. I was very bad earlier." He arched one eyebrow and looked at Annie, a teasing grin tugging at his lips. "Or maybe I was very good."

Annie groaned and shoved her way out of his arms. "Bad. You were bad."

Tyler moved just enough so she could squeeze by him, but she had to brush against him as she went. "It couldn't have been too bad—you kissed me back."

Annie ignored his comment and headed down the hallway to Courtney's room. She knew Tyler was trailing after them, but there was nothing she could do to stop him.

The man was almost as opinionated as her two-year-old daughter. And unfortunately, he was right. She *had* kissed him back. There was something about him that brought out the worst in her. His presence made her bad-tempered, which was surprising since she normally was slow to anger. But one look at Tyler could send her straight into orbit.

She turned on the clown light in Courtney's room and lay her daughter on the changing table.

"Can I help?"

Annie turned her head and looked at Tyler over her shoulder. "You know how to change a diaper?"

He laughed. "It's not exactly brain surgery. And I do have experience."

Annie frowned. "How come?"

"Not all of my friends dislike me as much as you do. I have done my share of baby-sitting over the years."

The thought of Tyler baby-sitting almost made Annie laugh. He was so big that she couldn't imagine him taking care of small children. He had to look like a giant to the little ones.

Tyler moved farther into the room. "So is it a yes?"

Annie kept her palm on Courtney's stomach and moved away a few inches. He was acting so strangely, almost like he was sincere. The Tyler Nelson she used to know would have never agreed to change a dirty diaper. Of course, that had been years ago, but still, he either had changed, or he was playing some new game on her.

"Are you sure you want to?"

"Yes." Tyler moved forward to replace Annie at the changing table. His presence delighted Courtney, who launched into a little nonsense song she sang when she was happy. Tyler kept up a string of compliments as he quickly removed the old diaper, cleaned her, and then taped the new diaper in place. Whatever else he'd learned over the last few years, he had indeed learned how to change a diaper.

"How was that?" he asked when he finished. He swung Courtney up into his arms. "I didn't do so badly, did I, precious?"

Courtney rewarded him with a sloppy, open-mouthed kiss. As it had in the grocery store a few days earlier, the sight of Tyler holding her child did strange things to Annie's insides. He looked so natural with the little girl propped on his hip, almost like he did it every day. Almost like Courtney was their—

Annie yanked her thoughts back to the present. "Thank you. You did a good job."

She picked up the old diaper and headed out of the

room while Tyler walked down to the bathroom and washed his hands. Now she knew for a fact that she'd lost her mind. How could she even think about Tyler being a father? Okay, so he knew how to change a diaper, but that didn't make him dad material. No, the man had broken her heart once, and she wasn't going to let herself fall for him again.

She'd learned from her mistakes all those years ago.

"So, do you think she'll go along with it?" Kevin asked.

Tyler glanced up as Kevin approached him outside. Dinner had gone better than Tyler had hoped. Of course, the fact that everyone there was on their best behavior had helped.

"I don't know. But I do think Annie's still mad at me." He took a long swallow of his iced tea. That was an understatement. Annie was furious at him, and he didn't blame her. He'd been teasing her since he'd seen her at the grocery store, but he just couldn't stop himself. The truth was, he was happy to see her, so happy that he'd pushed his way into her house tonight and brought his mother along just so she wouldn't throw him out.

For a few seconds, he'd thought she'd do just that when he'd kissed her. He'd been kidding and hadn't expected things to get out of hand. He certainly hadn't expected her to kiss him back. But she had, and he'd learned one thing—there was a lot more fire in Annie now than there'd been when they were kids.

But he didn't want a relationship; he wanted to make peace with Annie, and he hoped, be friends with her.

Kevin dropped into the lawn chair next to Tyler's. "Are you saying she's mad at you because she kicked you out here?"

When he'd offered to help with the dishes, Annie had reluctantly agreed. But when he'd placed a brief kiss on her shoulder once her hands were immersed in soapy water, she'd ordered him out of her house. With a shrug, he'd picked up his iced tea, taken Courtney by the hand, and come out into the backyard. At the moment, he was enjoying watching Courtney run across the yard chasing an imaginary bug.

"Annie resents what I did to her," Tyler said. "I don't blame her."

"But that was years ago. I'm sure she's over it by now."

Tyler shook his head. "I don't think so. And I'm more than a little sure she's going to go through the roof when she hears our plans."

Kevin's smile faded. "Yeah, I know. But this deal will be great for all of us—especially Mom and Dad."

"I know. But I understand how she feels. I hurt her when we were young. She's not about to trust me now, at least, not until I earn that trust again."

Kevin snorted. "So earn it. Do whatever you have

to do. Too much depends on this. Without your help, the expansion won't work."

Kevin wasn't telling Tyler anything he didn't already know, but it wasn't that easy. He couldn't just tell Annie to trust him. She needed time. And just because he was at the point where he was considering changing his life didn't mean that she was. There was a good chance she would hate him even more before the next few days were over.

It was getting so dark, he had trouble seeing Courtney. He stood and looked at Kevin. "I'll do what I can do. It just may take some time for Annie to adjust to the idea. I think we should've brought her in on the discussion from the start. I don't like going behind her back."

"If we'd told her up front, she would have tried to talk Dad out of it. Now that he and Mom are for it, there's not much Annie can do but accept our plans," Kevin said. "Tyler, I tried to find the money in other places, but I had no luck. And Dad deserves this. He's worked hard all his life. Annie can't let old disappointments ruin our chance at saving the business."

Tyler nodded. All Annie could do now was accept that he'd joined the business. Still, he felt bad knowing this deal would upset her.

With a final wave to Kevin, Tyler headed across the yard to lead Courtney back inside. He slowed his steps to let the little girl keep up with him. Boy, it felt wonderful being back in Summerly, seeing his friends and his family. Everything seemed cleaner here and felt more real. *He* felt cleaner and more real. Tyler glanced down at Courtney, who was concentrating on her walking. How could he have been so wrong for so many years? It seemed like he'd spent his life defending wealthy people who were guilty as could be. Some of the things they'd done had simply been misdemeanors, but over the last few years, their crimes had seemed to grow worse until he had thought he'd lost his soul along the way.

But now he knew he still had his soul. He stopped for a moment and looked at Annie framed in the kitchen window. She laughed at something her mother said, and Tyler couldn't remember ever seeing such a wonderful sight.

He'd missed this town. And deep down, he knew he'd missed this woman too. But his father may have been right. Maybe if he'd married Annie all those years ago, they wouldn't have been able to make that love last. Teenage infatuation tends to fade under the harsh reality of life. But he'd always liked Annie, long before he'd loved her, and he missed her friendship.

Tyler reached down and hoisted Courtney up on his hip. "I really like your mama," he told her.

She regarded him with a serious gaze. Then she stuck three fingers in her mouth.

Tyler laughed. "I really like you too."

Courtney nodded. "Man. Man," she said around her fingers.

Still laughing, he headed up the back stairs and into the kitchen. Annie turned and watched him walk in. He couldn't tell from her expression whether she was still mad at him, but if he had to guess, he'd say yes. If he was honest, he couldn't blame her for being mad. He'd pushed his way in here tonight, and even though she seemed to be enjoying herself, he knew he should have given her the chance to say no.

He'd just been afraid she would.

"I'll give Courtney her bath if you want," Tyler said.

Annie frowned. "I can do that."

Before he could say anything, Annie's mother, Fran, jumped in. "Didn't I teach you anything? Always accept any offers of help you get."

Annie stared at him, obviously debating what to do. Finally, she relented. "Okay, follow me. I'll show you where everything is."

Tyler bit back the grin threatening to cross his face. The last thing he wanted to do was gloat in front of Annie, but it still felt like a victory every time he managed to win even the smallest concession. He followed Annie back to Courtney's bedroom and waited in the hallway while she gathered up a new diaper and pajamas. Then he moved down the hall to the bathroom.

"Have you done this before?" she asked.

He smiled. He didn't blame her for being suspicious. He was the only child of two parents who were only children. He hadn't had much experience with children until a few years ago when his friends from college had started getting married and having kids. Since then, he'd spent a lot of time around children. He'd never thought he'd be the type to like kids, but he did.

"I told you I baby-sit. I mean it. If you don't trust me, stay and see." He moved past Annie into the tiny peach-and-aqua bathroom. Setting Courtney on her feet, he helped her pull off her clothes, and then he placed her in the small plastic bath seat. After he'd washed and rinsed her, he sat down on the tile floor to watch her play with an assortment of toys.

"You don't have to stay. You can get her out if you want," Annie said.

Tyler turned and looked at her. "I don't mind. She's adorable."

Annie still hovered in the doorway. He could tell she was reluctant to leave, and as much as he'd like to think it was his company she craved, he knew she stayed because she didn't trust him to watch Courtney closely enough.

He patted the floor next to him. "Want to sit?"

Annie moved slowly into the room. Instead of sitting on the floor next to him, she sat on the plastic child's stool in front of the vanity.

"You know, I can take care of her," he said. "I'm not going to let her drown."

"I'm not quite ready to turn the care of my daughter over to you," Annie said.

Tyler chuckled. No doubt about it, Annie was going to be a tough sell. He turned back to the tub and watched Courtney try to sink her toys. "She looks like you," he said.

Annie made a snorting noise. "No, she doesn't. But Mom says she has my temper."

Tyler glanced at Annie over his shoulder. As she watched her daughter, her face softened. She looked a lot like she had all those years ago. She was still as pretty as she'd been, but now she was older, wiser, and cautious.

When she saw him looking at her, she rubbed her hands on her jeans. He made her nervous, which wasn't what he wanted. He wanted Annie to trust him.

"So when are you going home?" Annie asked.

He liked that she spoke her mind. "Probably around nine."

"I meant back to New York. You can't stay in Summerly forever."

He hesitated for a moment. This would be the perfect time to tell her about the deal he'd worked out with her family, but he couldn't. When Kevin and Herb agreed it was time, they'd tell her.

"I haven't decided yet," he said. "Trying to get rid of me?"

She nodded. "Absolutely."

Courtney's fingers were wrinkled, so he put her toys away, let the water out of the tub, and picked her up. Wrapping her in a big blue towel, he dried her, then put on her diaper and pajamas. Throughout it all, Courtney giggled and babbled at him, and what little bit of his heart she didn't already own, she captured then.

"Mind shifting so Courtney can brush her teeth?" he asked.

Annie got a slightly mutinous expression on her face, but she didn't say anything. She stood and moved aside, so Courtney could climb on the stool.

"I take it the little toothbrush with the bear on the handle is hers?"

Annie sighed. "Yes."

He helped Courtney brush her teeth, then he combed her hair. When he'd finished, he was more than a little proud of himself. He beamed at Annie.

"So? Did I do okay?"

After a brief hesitation, Annie smiled at him. It was a small, somewhat polite smile, but it still counted. And it had a strange effect on his equilibrium. He took a step toward her, but she'd already turned her attention away from him and was hustling her daughter off to her bedroom. It was probably just as well. No sense muddying waters that were already too muddy.

He straightened the bathroom and turned off the light. As he walked toward Courtney's room, he could hear Annie singing softly to the little girl. Unable to resist the pull of her voice, he moved to the doorway and looked in. Annie had turned on the night-light and sat with her daughter in the big white rocking chair.

As she rocked, she sang to Courtney, who tried her best to sing along.

Annie looked up at him, her expression unreadable in the muted light of the room. He smiled at her. She smiled back. He should have felt fear, fear of falling for Annie all over again. Instead, he felt warmth. And he wanted to stay in that warmth. It was strange to think about changing his life. Over the last few weeks, he'd lost a lot of sleep struggling with the idea. But suddenly, it didn't feel so terrifying. It actually felt exciting. The future held promise. He felt certain if he tried and gave her time, he and Annie could probably be friends again.

He raised his hand in farewell and headed down the hall to get his mother. He needed to get home to check the e-mail from his office. Then he wanted to do some planning, so that when Annie found out he was buying into her family's business, he could give her some hard facts to back up the expansion ideas. He needed to have some ammunition in his corner to help her see their side of things.

And then she'd come around.

He grinned. Well, eventually she would.

Chapter Three

Something was wrong; Annie could sense it. All morning, her brother and father had been jumpy and distracted. Every time she got near them, they looked so guilty she would have thought they were planning something for her birthday if it hadn't been three months ago.

Plus, there was last night. When she'd finally gotten Courtney to sleep, she'd walked out into the living room and found the crowd gone, all of them, not just Tyler and his mother. Her own parents and brother had just left without even saying good-bye, which wasn't like them at all. Just like showing up at her house unannounced wasn't like them or laughing at Tyler's jokes wasn't like them.

So Annie knew without a doubt that something was

45

wrong. And whatever it was, she had a feeling Tyler was the cause of it. In fact, she was positive.

Finally, at a little after 10:00, she decided she'd had enough. One way or another, she was going to find out what was going on. She got up and headed over to the gray metal desk her father kept in the back room of the family's auto repair store. A middle-aged man sat in her father's chair, and as much as he looked like Herb Palmer, he couldn't be. The man behind the desk was humming, and her father never hummed.

"Okay, what's up?" Annie sat across the desk from her father, determined to get to the bottom of this.

"Hi, Cupcake. It's funny you should ask, because I've been wanting to tell you something." He fiddled with some pencils on his desk. Her father was a stocky man who always spoke his mind. His philosophy was to face the snake head-on before it caught him off-guard and bit him. But he didn't seem too interested in facing this snake.

Annie's stomach gave an uncomfortable lurch. "What?"

Herb smiled. It wasn't a normal smile. Rather, it was one of those too-happy smiles people had when they wanted to convince someone that something bad was actually good. Annie used that smile plenty of times when she needed to convince Courtney to eat something the little girl hated.

"I have some news," her dad said. "Nothing bad. Actually, it's good, very good. For all of us." He scratched the side of his face and avoided looking at Annie.

When he didn't say anything else after a few heart-stopping seconds, Annie said, "What? Tell me."

The pencils absorbed her father's attention again. "I think it's time for the business to expand."

"Expand?" She didn't like the nervous tremor in her voice, but she couldn't help it. Her father was taking so long to get to the point that she felt like she'd explode.

"Um . . . Yes. We have such a good reputation that I think we could open more stores."

This was the big secret? "Dad, expanding will cost a lot of money. I just finished the books for last month, and even though things are good, I don't think we have the capital to take on such a project. Unless, of course, we take out a loan."

"Well, there might be another solution."

Annie's nerves were shot. "What other solution?" she asked, feeling a sense of dread creep up her spine.

"Well, it's the funniest thing. Here I was thinking of expanding the business, and what do you know—Tyler's looking for a business to buy into. We'd be perfect for—"

Annie rose to her feet. She'd known Tyler's hand was in this mess. "You're kidding, right? You're not really going to take him on as a partner are you?" Her voice had risen as she'd spoken, so she made a conscious effort to get it under control again. "Dad, he can't be trusted."

Herb shook his head. "Nonsense. He's a great guy."

Annie blinked at her father. How could he say that? Just because they'd had one not-too-awful spaghetti dinner didn't undo the past. "Don't you remember what Tyler did?"

"That was a long time ago."

She took a deep breath and tried a different approach. "Dad, you can't be serious. Tyler can't invest in our business. This is the family's business—you, me, and Kevin—we run it together."

He again avoided eye contact with her. "Honey, that's been true up until now. But some things have changed lately."

Annie's stomach tightened even more. This conversation was coming at her from left field, and she felt completely unprepared for whatever it boded. She didn't like change. During the last couple of years, with the exception of Courtney's birth, change in her life was synonymous with disaster. Losing Paul had made every aspect of her life change, so now even small changes disturbed her. "What things have changed? Nothing's changed."

He shook his head slowly. "Sure they have. I'm not as young as I used to be. Your mother and I are thinking about retiring and having some fun. If Tyler buys my share, we can afford to do that. Plus Tyler has enough capital to underwrite the expansion, so you and Kevin will be better off."

That was it. Now she knew her family had gone insane. Her father hated free time more than anything in the world. He had to be right up to his elbows in work before he'd crack a smile.

"Retire and do what? You'll drive Mom crazy within a week. Plus, you'll just come in here, so why bother?"

Her father fiddled with the pencils again. "Well, we might not stay here. We might move."

"Move? Move where?"

Her father grinned a little-boy grin. "Oh, one of those warm places. Tahiti or someplace. Both your mom and I have had it with the cold. I don't want to shovel any more snow."

"Tahiti?" The knot in Annie's throat made it difficult for her to speak. She cleared her throat and tried again. "Tahiti's on the other side of the world. Kevin and I would never see you. Courtney's getting to the age where she appreciates having grandparents. You can't just leave."

Her father shrugged. "We haven't decided anything definite yet. Maybe we'll just spend the winters there."

How could her father say *Tahiti*, even in jest? If he really did intend to retire, the first thing she'd expect him to do would be to form a long-range plan for his future, something that would help him accumulate the necessary money to retire to someplace sensible—like Florida or Arizona—not Tahiti.

But she loved her parents and wanted them to be happy. "Well, I'm sure it will be awhile before you and Mom come to a final decision."

Again her father shrugged. "Not really. We love being around the family, but we'd like some time to ourselves too."

Annie stared at him. Since when did he and Mom want time alone? And since when was he a shrugger? Her father was a definite man, and definite men didn't shrug. They told you what things were and how they went, and that was that. There was no reason to shrug, no reason to avoid eye-contact.

No doubt about it—this was all Tyler Nelson's fault. Somehow he was behind the breakup of her family. That traitor had sat at her dinner table last night looking oh-so-innocent when all along he'd been planning the downfall of her family. He was a rotten rat. She needed to sit down with him and talk this over before he had a chance to do any real damage. For the moment, though, she needed to get her father off this subject.

"Why don't we talk some more this weekend at the house? Kevin and I can sit with you and Mom and talk it over. I'm sure you both would like some time to think about it."

"Oh no. We're sure this is what we want to do. But if you want to come over this weekend, that's great."

Her father stood. "I'll barbecue something on Saturday."

Thank goodness he'd finally said something that made some sense. If her father intended to drag out the old barbecue grill, then things were back to normal. He'd grill some steaks, and they'd all laugh about his even thinking he could retire anytime soon. Plus, he couldn't move. His whole life was in Summerly. He'd been born and raised here. His children had been born and raised here. His life was here.

"I think I'll see if your mother can make some turkey burgers," he said.

The warm, comfortable feeling that had settled over Annie evaporated, and her head snapped up. *Turkey burgers?* Her father was the cholesterol king. This was a nice change. She'd been trying to talk her father into watching his diet for years. "Turkey? That's great."

He nodded. "Yeah, the burgers are pretty good. Tyler showed us how to make them. He likes to spice his up, but I kinda like them plain. I thought they'd stink, but they don't."

"Dad, when did you see Tyler to have turkey burgers?"

"Oh, a couple of nights ago. He stopped over at the house and dropped off some oranges. He'd heard about my high cholesterol level, and he wanted to give us some ideas for new menu items that'd be easier on my arteries."

"How considerate of him," Annie said through gritted teeth. Of all the nerve of Tyler, suddenly appearing all over the place like some silly guardian angel, giving advice to her father, advice that included selling the store that he'd run for the last forty years. Oh, yeah, she could see it. Tyler would seem like such a great guy while he convinced her father to sell everything he'd worked for his entire adult life.

"Yeah, the burgers were good. Even Kevin liked them," her father said, oblivious to the effect his words had on his daughter.

"Kevin?" Annie's voice wobbled slightly. "Kevin was there too?" Up to this point, she'd assumed only her parents were involved in this plan. She'd hoped her brother would take the news the same way she had, and together they could persuade her father it wouldn't work.

"Sure. It was his idea that Tyler drop over in the first place. He knew I wanted to talk some business with the man."

It was now pretty obvious to her that this was going somewhere. The sooner they got there, the easier it would be on her nerves. "Dad, what's really happening? Don't pretend that for years you haven't had a thing about the Nelson family, because I know you have."

Her father waved his hand. "That's all in the past. I know now that Tyler was a kid and didn't mean to hurt any of us. Kevin's right—he's a great guy."

Somehow a lot of this conversation involved Kevin,

and her radar told her that sneaky brother of hers was a prime suspect. She stood and walked around the desk.

"Kevin certainly is something else," she muttered, not trusting herself to say more. She wanted to end this conversation before she said something to upset her father. Also, she wanted to hunt down her brother and find out what was really going on.

Her dad smiled. "Good. I told your mother you would be fine with Tyler joining the business, but you know how she worries. I knew you wouldn't still hold a grudge about something that happened so long ago."

Of course she wouldn't. She was practically a saint; at least her father talked as if she were. Why would she hold a grudge? Sure, he'd hurt her, but that was in the past. Her problem was that she didn't trust Tyler, not one little bit.

But she managed a smile for her father. Then she gave him a hug and set off to track down Kevin. He had a lot of explaining to do.

She finally found her brother in the storeroom re-stocking the spark plugs. Like Annie, Kevin had inherited their father's black hair and hazel eyes. He sat on a metal stool surrounded by cartons. He looked up as she approached, his initial smile replaced by a frown when he saw her expression.

"What's up?"

She sat on the stool next to him. "You tell me,

Kevin. Dad just explained he wants to retire, and he's asked Tyler Nelson to invest in the business."

Kevin's guilty look told her what she wanted to know. He was involved in all this right up to his eyebrows. What she didn't understand was why. Kevin had never been a friend of Tyler's, so why the sudden urge to go into business with him?

"Dad should have waited to talk to you about it. Nothing's definite yet," Kevin said.

"But you have been talking to Tyler, right?"

He nodded. "Yeah. He mentioned he wanted to invest in a business in town because he's thinking about moving back, so he can be close to his mom."

Annie sighed. "Well why would you want him to invest in our business? We're small. I'm sure Tyler wants something big."

"Not at all. And I explained that we were doing well, so it was the perfect time to consider expanding. Not only should we build a bigger store here, but we should also open another store across town."

How could her brother not see all the worms he'd let out of the can? Tyler Nelson wouldn't just buy into the business—he'd take it over. She and Kevin would be bulldozed at every turn. She looked into Kevin's face and knew he didn't see it that way. Despite his bulky size, Kevin was a sweetheart. He would never trample another human being, and to his way of thinking, neither would Tyler.

But Kevin didn't know the man. Tyler got what he

wanted in life, and in her experience, he didn't let much get in his way.

"Tyler may take over once he's bought in."

Kevin shrugged good-naturedly. "I don't see why he'd want to, but even if he did, I'm sure he'd make good decisions."

"Decisions you and I should make since we've worked here most of our lives."

Kevin frowned. "Annie, Dad's tired of working all the time. If Tyler buys in, Dad can retire. Also, if Dad does retire, that only leaves the two of us to run the business."

He left the sentence there as if she understood his point, which she didn't at all. "What's wrong with that? You and I know how to run this place blind-folded."

"If we want to stay small forever. But I'd like to see us become bigger. Tyler says that if we do it right, we can grow to three or four stores in five years. Think of it, Annie—we'd have stores all over the county."

She was thinking about it, and she hated the idea. "I like being part of a small, family-owned business where we know our customers."

Kevin bobbed his head. "Me too. But as Tyler pointed out, the days of the family business are behind us. A lot of small businesses have gone under recently. It's hard to compete with the big franchises."

"So what's your point—that if we don't become

big, we'll go under? That's silly. People know and trust us. We're doing great."

Kevin's expression hardened. "Not great enough. I want to do even better. I want us to grow, so we can hold our own against the big companies." He stood and dusted off the seat of his jeans. "Tyler's the way we can do it. He has the money. He knows how to run a business. You and I will be lucky if he decides to help us."

"Help us? You can't trust Tyler Nelson." She didn't mean to raise her voice, but she couldn't help it. Deliberately, she forced herself to take a deep breath and tried a different approach. "Besides, why would he even want to get involved with us? He's a hotshot lawyer."

"I think he wants to make a change."

Annie bit her lip. This wasn't getting her anywhere. Kevin's gaze was focused over her shoulder, but she didn't turn around. Instead, she stated her opinion as clearly as she knew how. "I don't like Tyler, and I don't want him within a hundred yards of this place. I'm going to fight you and Dad on this because I think it's wrong."

She turned to storm off to her office, but she faltered to a stop when she saw Tyler leaning against the doorway to the storeroom. Of course he was standing there. Today had turned out to be awful, so nothing should surprise her. And she knew from his expression that he'd heard everything she'd said.

Well, it was too bad. She'd meant every word, and it was just as well that he knew up front how she felt. Rather than being embarrassed, she tipped up her chin and met his gaze with a frosty one of her own.

"I mean it, Tyler," she said. She walked over until she stood directly in front of him. "Dad and Kevin may be buying your routine, but I'm not going to. I know what kind of person you really are."

She went to brush past him, but he refused to move out of her way.

"That was a long time ago," Tyler said. "I'm not the same person anymore. And neither are you."

"You're right about that. But this isn't about the past. This is about now, and I'm not going to let you ruin this business."

"Ruining it is the last thing I want to do."

"What about your real job?"

"As Kevin said, I'm interested in a change."

"Change somewhere else," she said. She pushed on his chest until he moved out of her way. Then she brushed past him and headed across the garage to her small office. She wasn't trying to be difficult. She just knew that Tyler wasn't a man of his word, so she would stop him somehow. No way would he get part of their business. At least, he wasn't going to without a fight from her.

"That went well," Tyler said dryly. He walked over to the stool Annie had just left and sat down. "So, what do you think I should do to change her mind?"

Kevin stood staring at the door his sister had walked through. He sighed and rubbed the back of his neck. "I don't know. She's really mad and really against the expansion. I thought she might be. That's why I put off telling her about it."

"How did she find out then?"

Kevin turned and looked at Tyler. "Dad told her this morning. He was all charged up, and I guess he thought she'd be happy or something."

"Which she isn't."

Kevin nodded. "Which she isn't."

"So how do we change her mind?"

"I don't know. I know I won't stand a chance. I'm just her brother. She never listens to a thing I say." He gave Tyler a long, assessing look. "But maybe you can bring her around."

"How? She doesn't trust me. You heard her."

"What I heard was Annie blowing off steam. She's mad that we've worked this out behind her back. Maybe we should have talked it over with her."

"She would still feel the same way. She doesn't like me."

Kevin chuckled. "For a smart man, you're pretty dumb sometimes."

Tyler wanted to argue the point, but he didn't have a lot to defend himself with. He did feel dense when it came to dealing with Annie. If there was a wrong way to handle the situation, he'd pick it.

"So what should I do now?" he asked.

Kevin shrugged. "I don't know—maybe sit down and talk to her."

Tyler sighed. Of course that was the best way to handle the problem, but he was very reluctant to do that. Annie would be difficult to convince, maybe even impossible. Still, he wanted this deal to work out, for lots of reasons, so he had to try. He stood and looked at Kevin. "If I don't come out of her office in fifteen minutes, call the police."

"Will do," Kevin promised.

As he walked to Annie's office, Tyler refused to listen to all of the self doubts floating through his head. His intentions were good, and all he had to do was get Annie to see that. He could do a lot for this business, and her entire family stood to profit nicely from his investment. All he needed to do was convince her to forgive him for the past . . . and trust him in the future.

That would be a tall order.

His little inner pep talk did nothing to raise his confidence. He tapped on the door to Annie's office and walked in without waiting for an invitation. He was fairly certain he wouldn't receive one anyway.

Annie looked up as he came in, a frown marring her features as soon as she saw him.

"I don't want to hear it," she said.

He dropped into the pale blue chair across the desk from her. "Tough. I want to talk about it."

She gave him a look that easily could melt the paint off a car. "Why are you doing this?"

"I'm not doing anything."

She leaned forward. "Oh, yes you are. First you try to get back into my good graces, then you decide you just can't live unless you buy into this business. Are you out to drive me crazy?"

He laughed, but his laughter died at the quelling look she gave him. He ran his hand through his hair. "Look, Annie, I know we've gotten off on the wrong foot. And I apologize for barging into your house last night. But I'm really not out to hurt you or your family. In fact, quite the opposite. I want to help the business grow."

"Why us? Why not just move your law practice here?"

The truth was the only answer he had. "I'm sick of practicing law. I want to do something different."

Her expression didn't soften. "What about your family? Isn't your mother upset that you'd buy into an auto repair store? Not too many years ago, the fact that my dad owned this place drove your family nuts. Remember that, Tyler? They hated that you wanted to marry an auto mechanic's daughter."

Tyler deserved that, and he knew it. "They were wrong then, and so was I. What can I do to convince you?"

"Leave us alone. That's what you can do for me."

He should have expected this. He'd done nothing

but manipulate Annie since he'd bumped into her, and dropping this bomb on her had to be a shock. The frustrating part was he actually thought he'd made some progress convincing her to trust him last night. She'd softened toward him as the evening wore on, but whatever ground he'd gained then was more than lost now.

"Annie, can't we be reasonable about this?"

Her eyes reminded him of the sea during a storm. "Why should I trust you? Why should I welcome you into this business?"

He played the only ace he had. "Because it's important to your father. He built this business. He made it his life. But now he wants something else, and you can give it to him. Don't you think he deserves some time off after all he's given you over the years?"

As he watched the pain form in her eyes, he knew it was a low blow. But it was also the truth. Herb Palmer wanted this to happen. The capital Tyler had would give Herb financial security. It also would more than allow the business to expand, so Herb's children would fare well in the deal.

That is, if they could get Annie to agree. At the moment, things didn't look so hopeful.

Her voice was tight when she finally said, "I need to talk to my parents some more. I haven't heard what my mother thinks."

Tyler nodded. "I understand." He stood and headed

toward the door, turning once it was open. "This will work out."

She looked at him blankly. "I'm not so sure."

Annie couldn't remember the last time her mother had looked so happy. Her smile was almost too big for her face, and Annie had the sinking feeling that her father's sudden decision to retire wasn't so sudden after all. Annie had decided to stop by during lunch and talk to her mother about the sale. But one look at Fran's face said it all. Like everyone else, she thought it was a great idea.

"Did they tell you?" her mother asked, that high-voltage smile of hers not wavering at all.

Annie nodded and wandered into the living room. As she sat in the chair facing her mother, that sinking feeling she'd had all morning kicked into overdrive. In some corner of her mind, Annie had thought she'd find an ally in her mother. "Yes, I know. But I'm not sure about this buyout."

Her mother's expression crumbled, and Annie felt like a heel. "You don't think it's a good idea?"

"No, I don't." Annie couldn't remember the last time she'd felt this guilty. But why couldn't any of them see how terrible this idea was? Tyler Nelson would ruin everything. Just by showing up in town, he'd caused trouble. Things had been perfect the way they were before.

"Why not?"

"Lots of reasons. For starters, he knows nothing about the business," Annie said, stating the most obvious and objective reason she had. "Have you and Dad had time to really think this through?"

"Yes, we have. You know, your dad's wanted to sell his part of the business for a long time. Tyler's the perfect solution—he's got the capital, and we know him."

"Mom, up until a few days ago, the only thing we knew about Tyler was he's the type to jilt his fiancée," Annie pointed out.

Her mother shook her head slowly. "That's not true. Tyler grew up here. We've known his family for years."

Her family had caught some sort of floating amnesia. None of them had a firm grip on the past. "His parents insisted he not marry me because I wasn't good enough for him."

The frown on her mother's face deepened. "I know he hurt you, honey. He hurt all of us, but he was a kid. Plus, this is different. This is business."

"I'm only mentioning the past because I think it shows the type of person Tyler is."

Her mother sighed. "Well, I'm sorry to hear you feel this way. I think the deal is already set. I told the boys they should talk to you first, but they didn't want to. Your father thought it would be better to just let you know once the plans were final."

And Annie knew exactly why they all thought that—

she'd object. Her father, her brother, and Tyler had known she would try to stop it.

Annie leaned forward in her chair and placed her hand on her mother's leg. "I'm not trying to cause problems. I just don't think now is a good time to change anything. Can't Kevin and I buy Dad out of the business?"

Her mother quoted a price that made Annie's blood chill. "Do you and Kevin have that much money?"

Annie didn't know anyone who had that much money. "Tyler's overpaying. The company's not worth that much."

"He's buying the reputation. Didn't they tell you he wants to expand?"

Annie started to tell her mother just what she thought of Tyler's plans, but the front door opened, and her father came in. He smiled at the women. Looking at Annie, he said, "I thought you might stop by here at lunch." He dropped down on the couch next to her mother and gave her a quick kiss.

"I wanted to know how Mom felt about your selling," Annie said.

"Did you know Annie's upset about it?" her mother asked.

"Still?" Her father looked so surprised that Annie almost laughed. It had been less than two hours since this bombshell had been dropped on her. It was hardly long enough for her to grow accustomed to the idea.

She tried one last time. "Are you really sure Tyler

is the right person to join our company? He knows nothing about the industry."

"But you and Kevin do. And Tyler can learn," her father said.

Well, that was that, Annie realized. Looking at the joy on her parents' faces reinforced what she already knew—the deal was done.

Annie sighed. "I just wish you'd discussed it with me earlier."

"Honey, we know how change upsets you," her mother said.

Annie nodded. Yes, they knew that, plus they knew she'd try to talk them out of it. But her parents looked so happy, she knew it would be selfish of her not to at least try to make it work. Even though she hated the idea of being in business with Tyler, she couldn't stand in the way of her parents' future. They deserved this good fortune.

So as much as she hated it, she'd just have to find a way to deal with Tyler Nelson.

Chapter Four

Tyler loved the smell of oil the way some people love the smell of apple pie. He'd never mentioned this to his friends because they'd think he was crazy, but it was true. The strong scent of engine oil immediately filled him with happy memories of the handful of precious days he'd spent over the last few years working on his classic cars. He didn't have the time needed to restore them himself, so he'd farmed the work out. But he still was as proud of his collection as a new father was of his baby. Now that he was back in Summerly and back at the house, he wanted to add to his collection.

Luckily, the garage at the house held six cars. With his mother's Lincoln, his Porsche, and his three collectible cars, he still had room for one more.

That was assuming Annie didn't run him out of town. Tyler knew she would let him have it when she returned from lunch. One thing about Annie—she wasn't shy about letting him know what she thought. Even when they were teenagers, she'd told him her opinions straight out without any sugarcoating. At that time, the girls at school had tended to fawn over him, so Annie's dead-on comments had been both annoying and intriguing. When it came right down to it, the reason he'd asked her out in the first place was because she wasn't impressed by his reputation. She'd seen him differently than other's had, which had been a daunting experience.

Tyler stood looking out at the cars in the parking lot when he saw Annie pull in and park her car at the side of the store. It was time for the battle. With a sense of dread, he walked into her office and sat in the chair facing her desk. He'd known all along that Annie would fight his joining the partnership, but now that it was time to deal with her anger, he was finding it difficult. He hadn't thought she'd still get to him after all these years, but she did. He liked the sparkle in her eyes and the sound of her laughter: Annie still had the power to kick his pulse into high gear. It put him at a disadvantage, which was something he wasn't used to.

He heard her speaking to some of the employees on the way to her office. She sounded friendly and happy, but he was fairly certain her attitude would change once she saw him.

"What are you doing here?"

He was right. Tipping his head, he smiled at Annie. She stood in the doorway, looking as if murder was the kindest idea she had in mind for him.

"Hi. How was your lunch?"

"Tyler, let it go. I don't want to talk to you right now." She walked by him and tossed her purse on her desk. "I've got a headache already, so I don't need another one today."

"I'm really not here to make life more difficult for you," he said, and he meant it.

"Can we talk about this tomorrow?" She sighed and sat in her chair. Even though she was as pretty as ever, she looked tired, and Tyler felt bad about that. He wanted to stand behind her and rub her neck and temples until her headache disappeared, but he knew better than to try. Instead, he chose a different approach.

"You know, you may find working with me won't be as terrible as you expect."

She frowned at him. "I don't mean to be rude, really, but I think we're just not made to work well with each other."

"You don't know that," he said. "We could be terrific together." Realizing what he'd just said, he hastily added, "Terrific together in business."

The look she gave him was doubtful. "Not if you insist on expanding until the company bursts at the seams. I don't think you have any idea how much work it takes to run this place. Kevin, Dad, and I are swamped all day long, and that's with ten employees working full time too."

"I'll pick up any work your father's been doing."

"So you'll go change the oil in a car if we get swamped?"

Tyler grinned. "Sure. I'd love it."

She made a noise that was somewhere between a snort and a huff. "I'll believe that when I see it."

"It's true. I'll do whatever I can to help."

Before he could add anything else, Karla, the receptionist, poked her head in the door and grinned at both of them. "Sorry to interrupt, but Doctor Dreamy is on line one for you, Annie." She winked at Tyler and then walked away.

Tyler wasn't surprised to see Annie glaring at him. Karla couldn't have picked a worse time to flirt with him.

"Don't you think she's kind of young for you, Tyler?"

He laughed. "I didn't do anything. She winked at me." Unable to stop himself, he added, "Can I help it if I'm irresistible?"

Expecting her to let him have it for that comment, he braced himself. But instead of getting angry, she simply sighed. "I'm too busy for this, and I have a phone call to answer."

He stood. "Who is Doctor Dreamy?"

Annie glanced at him, her expression blank. "Fred York. Not that it's really you're business, but he's someone I'm considering dating."

When he'd asked the question, Tyler had expected Annie to say something like he was Courtney's pediatrician, and that Karla just had a crush on him. The thought hadn't crossed his mind that this man might be Annie's boyfriend. Or maybe he wasn't her boyfriend yet, but he apparently wanted to be.

He couldn't stop himself from asking, "You're dating someone?"

"I'm thinking about it." When he didn't move, she raised one eyebrow and gave him a questioning look. "Would you mind leaving now, so I can answer the phone?"

"But we haven't finished our conversation yet."

"I imagine you and I will be fighting quite a bit over the next few weeks. We might as well declare today's skirmish over."

Of course, he wanted the fight to be over, but not just so Annie could take a phone call from some guy. "I'd like to try to clear this up now. Can't you call your boyfriend back later?"

"You're not going to leave, are you?" She didn't wait for him to answer. Rather, she picked up the receiver and punched a button on the phone. "Hi, Fred. How are you?" She spun her chair around, so her back was to Tyler.

He grinned. She was good. Still smiling, he sat back

down in the chair across from her. Buying into this business had been a smart decision, not only because he'd make a good profit on his investment, but also because he knew he'd have a terrific time doing it. Annie was enough to put zing in anyone's day.

Annie knew Tyler was still there. Just like when she'd been an infatuated teenager, she could sense Tyler Nelson from one hundred yards away. It wasn't just the faint trace of his cologne that lingered in the air, it was *him*. Too bad he was such a rat.

Fred was saying something about an operation he'd performed this morning, and she did her best to pull her attention away from Tyler and listen to him. Since Fred was a neurosurgeon, the specifics of the operation he'd performed were lost on her, but she still listened.

"I'm boring you, aren't I?" Fred said finally.

"No, I don't understand it all, but it's not boring."

"Why don't you tell me about your day?"

Annie smiled and glanced over her shoulder at Tyler. "How sweet of you to ask, Fred. My day has been rough. I've just learned that my father intends to sell his share of the business to someone I don't trust." Slowly, she spun around in her chair, so she could watch Tyler's face. "But let's not talk about that. Why did you call?"

She knew why he'd called, why he always called. Since she'd met Fred at a dinner party two months ago, he'd called her at least once a week to ask her out. Fred was a nice man—and Karla wasn't kidding—he was handsome. But Annie hadn't decided if she wanted to start dating yet. The thought of getting involved again bothered her. More than enough time had passed since Paul's death, but she wasn't comfortable with the idea.

That was before she'd had Tyler as an audience. The smug grin on his face made it impossible for her not to respond to Fred.

"I was wondering—" Fred started.

"I'd love to," Annie said. "Where and what time?"

Her answer obviously surprised Fred. It also had the expected result, Tyler's grin faltered and then faded.

Fred cleared his throat. "My partner is having a dinner party at the end of the month, on the twenty-seventh. How about if I pick you up at seven?"

Annie never moved her gaze from Tyler's face. "The twenty-seventh sounds fine with me. I'll see you then." After saying good-bye, she replaced the receiver and smiled at Tyler. "Why are you still here? Don't you have something better to do?"

He stood, his intense gaze never leaving her face. Finally he said, "Yeah, I think I do."

Tyler left her office without another comment, his usual flippant style repressed. Apparently she'd finally done what she'd wanted to do since she'd seen him in the grocery store; she'd knocked the wind out of Tyler's inflated sails. Her triumph should have made her feel great, but instead she was left with an empty sensation that had nothing to do with winning—and everything to do with losing.

"Courtney's cranky today," Ginny Adams, the director of Tiny Tots Day Care, said as soon as Annie entered. "She doesn't seem sick, just unhappy."

Ginny's announcement didn't surprise Annie. Nothing today had gone right. Why shouldn't Courtney be in a bad mood? And a two-year-old in a bad mood was like an earthquake during a hurricane. Courtney already became frustrated by the things she couldn't do yet, and she'd reached the age where testing limits was her full-time job. But for the most part, Courtney was a good-natured child. She might get upset for a while, but then she'd quickly get over it.

Annie could hear a child fussing down the hall, and she knew without asking that it was Courtney. When angered, her daughter would tell the people around her to "tak noff, ud," which was her way of imitating one of her uncle's favorite phrases he used when he drove: "Back off, buddy." At the moment, Annie could hear Courtney telling everyone to "tak noff," which didn't bode well.

"Maybe she'll settle down once I get her home and read her some of her favorite books. Sometimes that's all it takes," Annie said.

Ginny made a harrumphing noise that left Annie in no doubt as to what the other woman thought her chances were for a good night. But the most wonderful thing about a two-year-old was how quickly her moods could change. All Annie needed to do was find something to bring Courtney around.

When she entered Courtney's classroom, Annie quickly realized that "cranky" had been a nice description. Her precious daughter had red eyes from crying, and her bottom lip stuck out far enough to hang the proverbial cup on.

"Hi, Pea Pod," Annie said. She opened her arms and scooped her daughter up when the toddler ran to her. "What's wrong?"

Courtney launched into an explanation in which only every other word was decipherable.

"She's mad at Derek because he took the puzzle she was working on," Courtney's teacher, Julie, supplied. "After that happened, nothing calmed her down. Not even getting the puzzle back from Derek helped."

Annie nodded absently and put her hand on Courtney's forehead. Her daughter didn't feel hot, but she still might be sick, just not running a temperature. Annie cuddled the toddler closer, tucking Courtney's blond head under her chin. With a final good-bye, she left the day-care center and headed toward her car. Once Courtney was secured in her car seat, Annie climbed behind the wheel and adjusted the special mirror that let her see Courtney in the backseat. On the way home, Annie launched into her off-key rendition of "Old MacDonald," Courtney's favorite song. Courtney hesitated at first, but then she finally joined in. At the sound of her daughter's singing, the tight ball of tension in Annie's stomach relaxed. Thankfully, Courtney didn't seem sick. Plus, if Courtney was her normal, smiling self, then Annie would be able to unwind that night.

Boy, she certainly needed to unwind. Not only that, but she needed to decide what to do about work. It was obvious she had to find some way to be around Tyler without getting angry. The man meant nothing to her anymore, or at least, he *shouldn't* mean anything to her anymore. Despite the sizzling kiss he'd given her in her living room the other night, her only connection to Tyler now was business. She'd learned more than a few things over the years about separating one's personal feelings from one's business dealings. Now she just had to use that knowledge to handle Tyler. She could do this—she knew she could.

Her new resolve was put to the test when she swung her car into her driveway and had to hit the brakes to avoid rear-ending Tyler's gleaming Porsche. She parked her car next to his. Then, muttering, she turned off her car and shoved open her door.

"What are you doing here?" she asked him for the second time that day.

Tyler leaned against the side of his car, dark glasses covering his eyes.

"I need you to sign some papers." He pushed away from his car and walked down the gravel drive to stop near her. "I left you alone this afternoon because I knew you were too hot under the collar for us to have a rational conversation about this, so I waited until tonight." Tyler leaned over and waved at Courtney in the backseat. "Why don't I get her, and we can go over the papers in the house?"

Annie could feel her grip on her temper slipping by degrees, but she refused to give into it. Ever since she'd bumped into Tyler, she'd been behaving unpleasantly. Well, she wouldn't do it anymore. Granted, this opportunity to prove that she could handle a business relationship with Tyler had arrived sooner than she'd expected, but she could do this. All she had to do was put her mind to it.

With a small smile, she nodded. "Sure. Grab Courtney while I unlock the front door."

Her change in attitude obviously surprised Tyler because he stood still for a few moments, just looking at her. At least, she thought he was looking at her. With his dark glasses on, she couldn't be certain what he was looking at.

Without waiting to find out, she walked up the steps to her front door and unlocked it. Turning, she couldn't resist smiling at the picture she saw. Tyler sat in the backseat next to Courtney, his attention focused on unlocking the belt on the car seat. Courtney, on the other hand, apparently found Tyler's hair fascinating because she was pulling up small handfuls, making his short brown hair form little tufts around his head. Rather than getting angry, Tyler was laughing along with Courtney. After a few seconds, he unlocked the seat and freed Courtney. Annie watched them approach—the tall, handsome man with her small, plump daughter on his hip. They made a cute pair, especially since Tyler hadn't bothered to smooth his hair in place yet.

"Nice look," she said when he stood next to her on the porch.

Tyler grinned. "Do you think so? I told her she could play with my hair as long as she didn't pull it. It seemed like the best solution at the time."

Moving aside so Tyler could enter the house, Annie couldn't help marveling at how easily he'd turned Courtney into a sweetheart again. She definitely needed to have a talk with her daughter about men.

"So what are these papers you need me to sign?" Annie asked, forcing herself to pay attention to the reason for Tyler's visit.

Tyler sat Courtney down in the center of the living room. After the toddler ran off toward her bedroom, he turned to face Annie. "I know you don't like me joining the business, and I have to admit you've got good reason not to trust me."

A cold shaft of fear ran down Annie's spine. "I do?"

"Sure you do. I let you down once before. How do you know I won't do it again?"

Annie frowned. This had to be some sort of new kind of negotiating technique. Since when did one point out all one's flaws to an opponent?

"That's right. So, why are you saying this?" she asked warily.

"Because I want you to know that I understand it will take time before you can trust me again. I'm asking you to give me that time. Give me a few weeks, and if I haven't earned your trust, and you think the business has suffered, I'll sell my share to you and Kevin."

Stunned, Annie sank slowly into the plaid easy chair facing him. "You're kidding, right?"

He shook his head. "No, I'm not. I've given this a lot of thought, and I've come to the conclusion that nothing good can happen to the business as long as you and I are fighting. It's tough on us and everyone around us. So, for the sake of harmony, I'll make you this offer." He leaned forward, the expression in his green eyes deadly serious. "In return, I want you to let me have the time I need."

Annie studied his face, looking for a sign of insincerity, but she didn't find any. This deal sounded too good to be true. She would win either way. If Tyler didn't make a significant positive impact on the business within a few weeks, she could insist he sell his share. Or, at least, that was the way it sounded.

"I want some things clarified before I go along with this," she said, knowing she wasn't really in a bargaining position, but pressing her luck anyway. "First, how long is this 'few weeks?' "

Leaning back, Tyler watched her. "How long do you think is fair?"

He got her with the last word. What was fair? Fair to whom? If he was sincere, then all he wanted was a chance to earn a living in Summerly, and she couldn't blame him for wanting to return home. She'd experienced the same desire after Paul had died. She loved Summerly; the tree-lined streets, the aged buildings with their quiet dignity, and the scented air reminded her of simpler days and easier dreams.

But why couldn't Tyler find a different business to join? Why did he have to come back into her life after all these years?

"I'll give you eight weeks," she said, feeling more than generous. "During that time, you have to help us grow our business and not drive either Kevin or me crazy."

Tyler's face split with a grin. "Come on, what you actually mean is I'd better not drive *you* crazy. You know I don't bother Kevin."

She dismissed his point with a shrug. "Is that fair?"

"Eight weeks? I guess so. It's more than I expected you to give me."

Truthfully, it was more than she'd expected herself to give him too. But her conversation with her mother and father that day had proven to her that this was what they wanted. And even though Tyler Nelson was the last person she wanted as a partner, that's what he was—her partner. Her father and Kevin must have seen something in him that escaped her.

"For the sake of my family, I'm trying to be fair," she said. "But be forewarned—I'll fight you if you plan on expanding without doing your homework. Too many businesses go under when they take on too much too fast. Being a high-priced lawyer who drives a fancy car hardly qualifies you to run an auto repair store."

"I'm a quick learner, Annie. And I know enough about running a business to avoid the obvious pot-holes."

She wasn't sure he did, but she didn't argue the point. She wanted to go over more of the details of this deal, but it suddenly occurred to her that she hadn't heard a peep out of Courtney since they'd gotten home. She stood. "Tyler, do you mind waiting a minute? Courtney's been far too quiet for far too long."

"Sure. Take your time. I'll stay here and consider what I can do to make you trust me again."

This time don't leave. The words burned in her brain, but she didn't say them. Instead, she turned and headed down the hall to Courtney's room. Amazingly, the little girl was simply sitting on the floor in the middle of her room coloring in a book. Unfortunately, it wasn't a coloring book. Rather, it was the new romance novel Annie had bought yesterday.

"Oh, Courtney." Annie knew that to Courtney's

way of thinking, she'd done nothing wrong. After all, the book had been where she could reach it, and despite Annie's best efforts to find all the crayons and put them out of reach, apparently she'd overlooked this bright red one.

But since Annie wanted her book back without a fight, she might as well use Tyler as a distraction. "Hey, Pea Pod, want to go talk to the man? He's still here."

Courtney's blond head snapped up. "Man-man?"

Annie grinned. "Yes. Man-man."

Courtney dropped her crayon and scrambled to her feet. Without waiting for her mother, she tottered down the hall to the living room. Annie quickly grabbed her book from the floor and groaned when she flipped through and saw that most of the pages had been colored, but with effort, she could probably read the text.

She could hear Courtney in the living room talking to Tyler, or rather prattling at him, so Annie took the opportunity to go to her own room and put the book on the top shelf of her closet out of harm's way. She was on her tiptoes sliding the book on the shelf when Tyler spoke from directly over her shoulder, causing her to yelp and almost tumble over.

"What are you doing here?" Annie asked.

Tyler chuckled and reached out to steady her. Even though he only had his hand on her elbow, the contact was too personal, and Annie pulled away quickly.

"You know, you've spent most of the day asking me that question," he pointed out.

Annie tugged self-consciously on her skirt. The closet in her bedroom was hardly the place where she wanted to have a conversation with Tyler. "Well, I keep asking because you keep turning up in places you're not supposed to be."

Tyler raised an eyebrow. "Oh, really?"

As her gaze met his, the air between them seemed to crackle with awareness. And she knew the gleam in his green eyes meant trouble. With a self-will she didn't know she possessed, Annie pushed past him, needing to put some space between them. Wanting something else to think about other than how Tyler Nelson made her feel, she glanced around her bedroom. "Where's Courtney?"

"Watching a tape on TV. She told me she wanted ink, so I thought I'd come get you to find out what that means."

The smile on Tyler's face made Annie wonder how she was going to work with him if every time he came near her the tension level in the room skyrocketed.

"That means she wants something to drink. I probably should start dinner." She glanced briefly at him, wondering if he expected her to invite him to stay. But she wasn't going to. The time they'd spent together so far had been infuriating, and taxing, and in the case of the kiss the night before, upsetting to her equilibrium. She needed some time to think through what had happened.

Tyler shut the door to her closet and then leaned back against the wall. She watched him make a slow perusal of her bedroom, his deep green eyes lingering longer than she liked on her queen-sized bed. She braced herself for some comment, but he made none. Instead, after a moment, his gaze returned to her face.

Annie felt another jolt of awareness and knew she wasn't imagining it. Whatever had existed between Tyler and her all those years ago still existed. In fact, it seemed much stronger now that they were adults than it had when they'd been a couple of kids necking in Tyler's car. This was the reason he made her so mad, the reason she'd been avoiding him whenever possible, and the reason she didn't want to work with him.

Because whether she liked it or not, the bottom line was that she was every bit as attracted to Tyler Nelson now as she'd been when she'd been a naive teenager in love with the town's fair-haired boy.

Annie forced herself to glance away, breaking the spell that had settled over the room. "Why don't we go check on Courtney," she mumbled, heading toward the door.

Tyler placed his hand on her arm. "We should . . ."

She looked up at him, willing him to understand that this spark between them wasn't something she wanted in her life. It wasn't something she could deal with at this moment. She'd loved Paul deeply, and being a widow was so difficult at times, she wanted to scream. But getting involved with Tyler wouldn't help anything. It would just make everything worse.

Tyler must have seen the fear in her eyes, because he dropped his hand from her arm and stepped away. Wordlessly, Annie left the room and headed toward the sound of the TV.

"Now what about those papers you need me to sign?" she asked when she reached the living room.

For a moment she thought Tyler would push her about what had almost happened in the bedroom, but he didn't. Instead he pulled some papers from the pocket of his jacket.

"These papers pertain to the sale of Herb's part of the company. You need to look them over, so you'll understand what this means."

"I already understand what this means. It means you own exactly as much of the company as Kevin and I do. And it means that you get to devise a job for yourself at the company and draw the same weekly salary as Kevin and I do."

"True, but it also means that I don't have to make the agreement I made earlier with you. I don't have to abide by your eight-week limit. I'm doing it because I want to make you happy."

Now *there* was a joke. Annie smiled ruefully and shook her head. "No, you don't want me to be happy;

you want yourself to be happy. You want me to stop fighting you. Your offer is in your own best interest."

"And yours too."

"Maybe. It is if you live up to all your promises and help this company rather than hurt it. If you don't, then by agreeing to give you eight weeks, I've given you carte blanche to run the company into the ground. The way I see it, I've got a lot to lose."

Her comment obviously bothered Tyler because he ran an agitated hand through his hair. "Why can't you just let this work? Why do you have to keep looking for the worst in me?"

"Because I'm afraid of you," she admitted. "You have too much power and can do so much harm."

"But I won't," he said softly. He moved forward a few steps, so he stood directly in front of her. She had to tip her head back to see his face. In the background, she could hear the singsong music of Courtney's videotape, but slowly the music faded, and she was only aware of Tyler. For a second, she felt the same tension she always felt around Tyler. Automatically her gaze dropped to his mouth. It was full and firm, and she remembered too well the feel of it against her own.

Tyler lifted his hand as if he intended to cup her face, and for a moment, Annie wanted him to. She wanted him to kiss her again.

Tyler leaned toward her. "I won't hurt you," he said.

His words broke the spell. "You already did a long time ago."

With somewhat jerky movements, she took the papers from his hand, stepped away from him, and headed toward the front door. She opened it slowly and waited patently for him to leave. Not once did she meet his gaze as he gave Courtney a quick hug and then walked across the room to where she stood.

When Tyler reached her, he stopped.

"I'm not a kid anymore. I don't make the same kinds of mistakes I used to," he said. "You have to know I'm sorry I broke my promise to you."

Annie finally met his gaze. "I'm not a kid either, and like you, I don't make the same kind of mistakes I used to make—like trusting you."

"Are you really sure that was a mistake?" he asked. Without waiting for her to answer, he walked out the door. He didn't look back.

Chapter Five

Tyler knew there had to be a way to make this work. He'd honestly thought his offer to sell back his part of the business would give Annie all the reassurance she needed. Obviously, he'd been wrong. He knew she wasn't upset about the past anymore. Annie was a fair person, and even though his stupid mistake might have left a bad taste in her mouth, she wouldn't hold it against him after all these years.

If she wasn't holding the past against him, then she was holding the future . . . or at least the future she thought might happen if he expanded the business. And he dearly wanted to expand the business. Palmer Automotive could grow into something formidable if they just had the courage to let it happen. He'd done the research. It would work.

But Annie might not let it happen.

"What are you doing sitting in the dark?"

Tyler turned and looked at his mother for a second before she turned on the light in the study. He blinked against the sudden brightness.

"I'm thinking," he said.

Marguerite walked into the room, her floor-length satin robe making her look regal. She sat on the cream sofa facing his chair. "Is this something you can discuss with your mother?"

He smiled. It was nice being home, having someone care if he was worried. He'd spent so many years in a city filled with unknown faces that it felt comforting to be somewhere where he had connections.

"Annie's not happy that I'm joining the business," he said.

His mother nodded. "Which you knew would happen."

"True, but I thought she wouldn't want me to join because of the past, but that's not it. She doesn't want me to change things."

"Which you will," Marguerite said.

"Which I will." He sighed and rested his head against the back of his chair.

"And that bothers you?"

"Well, I don't want to upset Annie."

His mother's green eyes narrowed. "And why is that? Why do you care if this upsets Annie?"

Now there was a good question. He thought about

it for a moment, floundering for an answer. Finally he gave his mother the only answer he could think of. "Because I like Annie."

"Like her how?"

He chuckled. "Not the way your tone is implying. I just mean that I like her as a person, so naturally I don't want to upset her."

"But this is business." His mother's words were clipped and brisk, a fair imitation of the tone his father had always used when he'd discussed business.

"I think you listened to Dad too much," Tyler said with a chuckle.

Marguerite folded her hands across her lap, looking every bit as elegant as she had years ago when their house had been filled with corporate officers and politicians. "Your father was an excellent businessman."

"And everything was business to Dad, wasn't it?" Tyler didn't mean his question as an accusation, but when his mother stiffened, he knew she'd taken it as one.

"Henry worked hard for everything he received. When success doesn't come easily, one tries harder to hang onto it."

"And success came easily to me, didn't it, Mom?"

She smiled slightly. "Well, let's just say that we invested a great deal in silver polish to keep your spoon shiny."

Tyler laughed. "It's nice to know you think I was spoiled."

"Your father and I wanted the best for you." Her smile slowly faded. "Maybe we didn't make all the right decisions, but our intentions were good."

This conversation had taken an unexpected turn, but Tyler had supposed it would have been only a matter of time before they discussed the past. "Do you think I blame you for something?"

"Don't most children blame their parents for past mistakes?"

"Maybe. But I'm sure once they have their own children, they realize how difficult being a parent is." He leaned forward and laid his hand on his mother's knee. "I know you and Dad meant well. I'm grateful for everything you did for me while I was growing up. My life is easier because of you."

Marguerite blinked several times, and Tyler knew her eyes had filled with tears. "Now how did we get on such a serious topic?"

Tyler leaned back. "Annie. We got here because of Annie." He was sorry he'd made his mother cry, but they needed to talk about this since he was now in business with Annie and her family. "Does it bother you that I've bought into Palmer Automotive?"

Her mother stared at him. "Of course not. Why would it bother me?" Before Tyler could answer her, she said, "I see. Because of the past. But you're not the only one who has grown wiser with age. I'll admit your father and I made some mistakes, and I now know we shouldn't have interfered in your relationship with Annie."

Tyler couldn't stop himself from asking, "So why did you?"

"Because you both were so young." She sighed. "We wanted you—and Annie—to explore the world and go to college before you made a enormous decision, such as marriage."

Tyler thought about what she'd said, and she was right about one thing; they'd been very young. "Well, it was a long time ago."

"Yes, it was. But I want you to know I like Annie a lot, and her family. I think your buying into the business is a terrific idea."

"If only I could find a way to convince Annie that it's terrific. There's so much we can do with the company if she'd just let us. Kevin's interested, but I won't gang up on her."

"So do what you do best."

Tyler couldn't resist the bait. "And what would that be?"

"Dazzle her like you do the juries. You wouldn't have done as well as you have if you hadn't learned how to get people to see your viewpoint. Let's face it, you're a good lawyer because you're good at convincing people to change their minds."

His mother definitely had a point. He seemed to instinctively know how to read people and figure out what they needed to hear to make them understand his way of thinking.

And it was easy to see what Annie needed—she needed security, she needed consistency. She needed something to believe in.

So he had to show her he was that something.

"Now I know where I got my brains," Tyler said to his mother with a smile.

Marguerite stood and headed toward the door. "Not only your brains. I'm also responsible for your good looks." She waved at him as she walked out the door, leaving her son laughing behind her.

No one had ever sent Annie flowers at work, never. Even when Paul was alive, she'd never received flowers.

But she had today. At a little after ten, Karla came into Annie's office carrying a huge bouquet of flowers. It covered Karla's face, and Annie rushed over to help the receptionist before she smashed into the wall. Together, the two women set the flowers on her desk.

"I guess I don't have to ask how your night was." Karla giggled, her fingers touching the petals of one of the many red roses in the arrangement.

Stunned, Annie just stared at the flowers. "These are for me?"

Karla picked the note out of the holder and handed it to her. "I think Doctor Dreamy is really stuck on you."

"Why would Fred send me flowers?" This had to be a mistake. They weren't going out for several weeks. Granted, Fred had been after her for a long time to go out with him, but a simple yes didn't deserve a gesture this extravagant. She pulled the card out and turned it over.

"So what does the dear Doc have to say?" Karla leaned toward Annie.

"They're from Tyler." Annie set the card on her desk and then returned to her chair.

"Tyler?" Karla picked up the card and laughed. "Thanks for the eight weeks." Frowning, she looked at Annie. "What does that mean?"

"It means I'm in for a long couple of months." She didn't add anything else, and eventually Karla figured out that was all she intended to say.

Karla slipped the card back into the holder nestled among the flowers. Then, with a shrug, she left Annie's office, no doubt so she could tell everyone else about the flowers.

Annie studied her present. She really shouldn't have been surprised that Tyler had done this. The flowers didn't mean anything, at least not in the romantic sense. But Tyler had made no secret of his desire to win her over to his side. No doubt this was one way that had worked well with the women he had known in the past.

Still, in some strange way, his gesture tugged on long-buried emotions. Sighing, she sat behind her desk. What was it about Tyler that threw her into a tailspin? Probably it was the mesmerizing effect he had on her. When he looked at her with that heated gaze of his, she felt like a teenager again. He'd been the best-looking boy she'd ever seen, even if he was too cocky for his own good. Time had turned him into the best-looking man she'd ever seen.

And he was still as cocky as ever. This was all so confusing. She hadn't expected to ever feel this way again about a man, especially Tyler. He'd been wrong for her all those years ago, and he was wrong for her now. Paul had been so steady, so practical. Falling in love with him had been slow and gradual, the kind of love that would last a lifetime. Had Paul lived, she was certain they would have continued to enjoy the peaceful, comfortable love they'd always known. In the two lovely years they'd had together, they'd hardly ever disagreed. They'd been so much alike, they seldom differed in their opinions.

Annie ran her fingers through her short hair in aggravation. Now why couldn't Tyler be like that? She wouldn't mind his joining the business if he was reasonable. But he loved playing the maverick, and he wouldn't be happy until he'd turned everything in the business upside down.

"Did someone die around here?"

Annie glanced at the door. Kevin leaned against the jamb, his wary expression belying the humor in his words.

"It's early in the day yet. Who knows how it might turn out," Annie said ruefully.

Kevin came into the office and dropped into the chair across from her. Leaning forward, he placed his hands on his knees and stared at her.

"Dad isn't coming in today. He told me last night that he and Mom are going to the travel agent to plan a trip."

A sadness crept through Annie. Although she was happy for her parents, she'd miss having her father at work each day. This part of her life was over, and she was uncertain as to what the future held. "Are they going to Tahiti?"

"Yeah. I think so."

Drumming her fingers on the wooden top of her desk, Annie studied her brother. "You know I'm upset with you."

Kevin laughed. "Yeah, I know."

"But do you understand why?"

"Sure. You hate Tyler."

"No, that's not it. I'm upset because I deserved to be involved in this decision. You and Dad snuck around me like I wasn't even part of the business, and I resent it."

Kevin had the decency to look embarrassed. "I know we should have told you. Dad said several times that it was wrong to just spring the deal on you."

"Dad was right."

"Ah, Annie, you know how you are about changes

sometimes." Kevin shrugged. "Can we just let it go and move on? Tyler's already given Dad the money. We can't back out now."

Annie struggled to keep her tone even. "Yes, I know. But I need you to promise that from now on, I'll be included in all major business decisions. That's not negotiable. I'm part of this business, and you and Tyler are going to treat me as such."

Before Kevin could answer, Tyler appeared in the doorway looking tan and fit and unbelievably handsome. Annie shifted her gaze to him. "Did you hear that?"

He moved farther into the room, his penetrating green gaze making a slow flush creep across her cheeks. The more time she spent around him, the more intense her attraction for him became. Despite all the reasons she had for disliking him, she just couldn't do it. He made her feel alive, something she hadn't felt in years. Her heart raced so fast, she felt like she'd just sprinted around the parking lot. A slow smile crept across his lips, and seemingly without will, she smiled back.

"You boys have to agree not to go behind my back anymore."

Kevin grinned. "Does that mean you've forgiven me?"

"Yes." She gave both men a stern look. "But that's it. Never again."

Kevin drew a cross on his chest. "Cross my heart."

Annie shifted her gaze to Tyler. "What about you?"

"I promise. Have you changed your mind about the eight weeks?"

"No. You made the offer, and I plan to take you up on it."

Kevin glanced from Annie to Tyler and back again. "What's she talking about?"

Tyler's gaze never left Annie's face as he answered, "I promised her that I'd sell my share of the business back to the two of you if she's still unhappy with me at the end of eight weeks."

Kevin made a choking noise and rose to his feet. "You're kidding, aren't you?" His gaze flew to his sister's face. "Annie, you can't make him do that. We need him—"

"Actually, you only need my money, Kevin. You don't need me."

Kevin ignored Tyler. "Annie, you're ruining everything. This is the chance of a lifetime for the two of us. We're incredibly lucky that Tyler was even willing to consider joining the business. I'm sure a lot of other people in this town would have given anything to have him as a partner."

Struggling to keep a lid on her temper, Annie stood. "All I'm asking is to have a voice in future changes."

Kevin moved forward until only her desk separated them. "I went behind your back because you act so weird every time anyone suggests making even the smallest change. You've been so jumpy since Paul died."

Annie felt his words like a blow. "This has nothing to do with Paul."

Kevin sighed. "Of course it does. Everything with you does. Paul died, and now you can't handle having anything else happen to your world. Well, change happens whether you like it or not."

Annie's frustration boiled over. "What do you know about change, Kevin? You've never left the town you were born in. You went to work for Dad as soon as you left college. You don't know what it's like to lose everything."

Kevin slammed his fist down on Annie's desk, making her jump. "Neither do you, Annie. You lost Paul, not everything. You still have Courtney, you still have a family, you still have a job. But you may not for long, if you keep acting like this."

"Kevin, back off," Tyler said.

Her brother spun his head around and stared at the other man. "You know it's the truth. She has to face reality even if it means we have to shove it in her face."

Annie's chest felt tight, and she willed herself to relax. Stress always got to her like this. She hated being backed into a corner. Even though Kevin's words hurt, Annie knew she had to have this out with her brother. Too much had happened for them to pretend things hadn't changed. The last few days had rocked her world out of kilter, and nothing she did seemed to steady it.

"Okay, Kevin, spit it out. What reality do I have to face?"

"The business is dying, Annie. We can no longer compete with the big companies."

"What are you talking about? I do the books. Things are fine. We haven't had a drop in revenue or in our customer count."

"But we will unless we expand, so we can compete with the big guys. Soon we won't be able to meet their prices because we can't buy in bulk. And our services won't meet theirs either unless we update our equipment. So we either let Tyler join this business, or we close the doors and hang up the closed sign before we go broke."

Could she really have been that blind? How could something like this be true without her noticing?

"You never said anything. Surely, you and I could—"

"We don't have enough money, Annie. I just built my house two years ago before those franchises opened out by the highway. I've got bills I have to pay."

And so did she; Paul's insurance hadn't been much, and she depended on her salary to live. Kevin was rarely serious and almost never angry, but today he was both. And she knew that meant he was telling her the truth.

"Why didn't you tell me sooner?" she asked.

"Because so much had already happened to you that Dad and I didn't want to dump this on you too. Up until recently, we hadn't a clue about what to do." He drew a deep breath. "Then Tyler stepped in."

Annie glanced at Tyler. Rather than looking pleased at how this conversation was going, he looked uncomfortable.

"So in reality, you're the cavalry, right?" Annie asked him.

Shaking his head, Tyler moved over to stand next to Kevin. "No, I bought in because I wanted to find something in Summerly that I could be a part of."

Annie studied him. "You're definitely staying in town? You're not going back to your law practice?"

Tyler didn't answer her at first. Finally, after several long moments, he said, "I've taken an extended leave from the firm."

"So you may go back?" Annie knew she was pushing, but she needed the facts. "Even before the eight weeks is up?"

"I really don't know right now, but if I do, I won't leave you and Kevin in the lurch. I'd only leave once things are settled about the expansion. And I wouldn't sell my share. I'd become a silent partner."

So he might leave again. Funny, Annie knew that knowledge should have brought her some degree of satisfaction, but it didn't.

"I see," she said slowly, pushing aside the emotions

tumbling through her. "Well, while you're here, I'd like you and Kevin to stop treating me like I'm made of china." She shifted her gaze to her brother. "For starters, I need to know what's happening. As you pointed out, I depend on this place to live, so I refuse to be left in the dark."

"You're right," Kevin said. He looked at Tyler and then back at her. "I promise I won't do it again."

For the first time since Kevin had lost his temper, Annie felt the pressure in the room lighten. At least now she knew the truth. She also knew that Kevin was afraid she couldn't take reality. But she wasn't as delicate as everyone thought. Still, she needed to try harder to let people know she wouldn't break. And maybe she needed to try harder to let herself know that too.

She looked at her brother, loving him for his intentions despite his actions. Other than the natural squabbles between siblings when they were growing up, the two of them had always gotten along well. She couldn't remember a time when Kevin hadn't been on her side. He wouldn't start misleading her now.

"I'm not about to promise to stop fighting you." When both Kevin and Tyler frowned, she continued on. "Not if you suggest something I think is wrong. But I will agree to work with you to reach solutions to our problems." She turned her attention to Tyler. "I know now that we need to make some changes, but I'm not willing to make any until we do some real research. I think we need to know what we're up against before we start changing things."

The tightness in the muscles in Tyler's face made it clear that he didn't like her approach. Before he could say anything, Annie pushed on.

"I know you two think I'm saying I don't want to even consider changes. That's not true. But I want what we do to actually help. If we choose the wrong actions, we might make things worse."

"Kevin and I have done some preliminary work," Tyler said. "I'd be happy to go over it with you."

Annie bit back the retort that hovered on her lips. Several seconds ticked by while she considered Tyler's offer. One thing was certain—she didn't want any more cozy little meetings like the one last night. She had enough problems keeping her mind off Tyler without finding herself alone with him in close proximity.

"I have some time this afternoon if you want to go over it here."

A teasing smile hovered around Tyler's lips. "Truthfully, today is bad for me."

Here it comes. Annie braced herself for his suggestion, knowing it would be something she'd need to veto.

"Why don't you come to dinner tonight at my mother's house? Mom would love to see Courtney again."

His offer caught Annie off-guard. She'd expected

him to ask her to dinner, but not at his house with his mother there. "Are you sure? Courtney's a handful, and your mother's been sick."

Tyler shook his head. "Mom and our housekeeper, Dolores, have been hounding me to have you over, so I know they'll be thrilled. After dinner we can take a few minutes to go through what I've found out so far." He took a deep breath, as if steeling himself to press on. "I also have some suggestions I'd like to make."

Annie straightened. Suggestions? Well, she had to find out about them sooner or later. It was important for her future, and more important, for Courtney's future.

"Fine. What time should we come over?" Annie asked.

"Why don't I pick you up at six?"

"In your Porsche? I don't think so. I'll drive over." Hoping to prevent an intimate meeting, she turned to Kevin. "You should be there too."

Kevin didn't look at her. Instead, he seemed fascinated by something on the floor. "I've already heard Tyler's suggestions."

"Naturally," she said dryly. Turning back to Tyler, she said, "Okay, I'll come over a little after six."

Tyler opened his mouth as if to argue, but then he abruptly said, "Fine."

Kevin used the break in the conversation to mutter something about ordering fan belts and quickly escaped her office. Once he was gone, Tyler stepped over to the desk and lightly touched the flowers.

"I hope you like these."

"Of course. They're beautiful. But I'd rather you didn't do something like this again."

"You seem in the mood to issue ultimatums to me today. You know I never follow directions very well." Without waiting for an answer, Tyler grinned at her and then walked out. Annie stared at the space where he'd been. The man would drive her crazy. What bothered her most about working with Tyler wasn't any changes he might have in mind. What she really feared was her attraction to Tyler, a man who was—and had always been—wrong for her.

When Karla appeared in the doorway a few minutes later, Annie welcomed the interruption. Everything that had happened that morning had thrown her day off.

"So, isn't Tyler a sweetie? And he's so cute! I'd give anything for him to ask me out."

As Karla's words sunk in, Annie turned to look at the younger woman. Maybe this was the solution to her problem. If Tyler was interested in someone else, Annie could finally convince herself to stop thinking about him. "Why don't you ask him out?"

A wary expression crossed Karla's pretty face. "Do you really think I should? I mean, he might say no."

"But he might say yes. You'll never know if you don't ask." It was odd having this conversation with

Karla. She'd always thought of the receptionist as the daring sort who wasn't intimidated by anything. Apparently some things bothered everyone, no matter how brave they might appear to be. Annie leaned forward, caught up in the discussion. "And as you said, he's nice, so I'm sure he won't mind."

Indecision covered Karla's face. "To tell you the truth, I've never asked a guy out before." She grinned. "I've never had to. Usually they get the hint to ask me."

"Then maybe it's time you did the asking. Why should men always be the ones to ask? Why should they always be the ones who make the decisions? It's wrong. They shouldn't have all the power. We women need to take control. I think—"

"Whoa!" Karla waved her hands in surrender. "Gosh, you're getting so upset, you'd think this was about you rather than about me."

Annie drew in a shaky breath. She'd gotten carried away there, but why shouldn't Karla ask for what she wanted in life just like Tyler did?

And why shouldn't I? a little voice murmured in the back of Annie's brain. But she ignored the voice and dealt with the problem at hand.

"So? What do you think?"

Karla nibbled on her bottom lip. "I don't know. I don't want to give him the wrong impression. He might think I'm chasing him. Some men don't like pushy women."

"You're not being pushy. You're just letting him know you like him."

A variety of expressions crossed Karla's face, and as they did, Annie considered her own motivation. As much as she hated to admit it, she wasn't doing this just as a favor to Karla. She wanted Tyler involved elsewhere for her own purely selfish reasons, especially after today. He'd told her he might leave again. Annie had lived through that experience once before. She couldn't risk falling for Tyler again only to have him walk out on her. She needed to keep her attention focused on the business. They had to make careful changes or there might not be a business left for any of them to work for.

Annie glanced at Karla. The receptionist was a nut in many ways, but she had a good heart. Annie felt compelled to issue at least a token warning. "You know, Tyler mentioned he might leave town again. I'm not sure he plans on staying here forever."

Karla giggled. "I'm not looking for forever, Annie. I was thinking more along the line of some fun dates."

So much for her worrying about Karla. "Well, then I think you've found the right guy."

"Good," Karla said. "There's nothing I hate more than a boring date."

"So are you going to ask him out?"

Since she was fairly certain Tyler and Karla would

be perfect together, Annie decided to play devil's advocate.

"What's the worst thing that could happen?"

That seemed to stump Karla. She shrugged. "I don't know. Maybe I completely humiliate and embarrass myself, and then I have to face him every day knowing he turned me down."

"So what? What difference does that make? Your self-esteem shouldn't depend on whether Tyler Nelson wants to date you or not. If he says no, then it's his loss."

Her argument seemed to convince Karla. Her head bobbed in time with Annie's words. "You're right. I think I will ask him. I mean, if he doesn't want to, all he has to do is say no."

Annie nodded. "Absolutely."

Smiling, Karla headed toward the door. Just as she was about to leave, she turned to look at Annie. "Thanks. You're the best."

Annie groaned as the young woman walked away. "No, I'm not," she muttered. She was a louse. Although it was true she thought there was nothing wrong with a woman asking a man out, Annie knew she'd pushed Karla harder than she should have. She'd pushed because she was afraid of her own feelings. She remembered all too well what it felt like to be kissed by Tyler. In the last few days, she'd day-dreamed about him more than once.

She'd pushed Karla out of fear, fear of her own

emotions. Ever since Tyler had returned to town, she seemed to be turning into someone she didn't know.

Worst, a little voice kept asking her a question she wanted to ignore—how would she feel if Karla really did ask Tyler out and he said yes?

"Why is life so complicated?" Annie muttered as she fumbled in her desk drawer for her aspirin bottle. Today promised to be another long day.

Chapter Six

"You know Annie and I can't buy you out. Neither of us has that kind of money," Kevin said the second Tyler walked into the storeroom.

Tyler pulled up a metal chair and sat. He waited until the sound of an air wrench being used in the garage died down before he said anything. "I don't expect you to buy me out. Like I said, I can become a silent partner."

Kevin looked at him as if he'd lost his mind. "Then what will you do, just sit around and grow old?"

"No. I'll go back and practice law."

"I thought you hated being a lawyer."

"I don't hate it. I just don't enjoy it as much as I used to." Truthfully, he didn't know what he wanted to do about the practice, but he had to decide. Maybe it was cowardly of him, but in a way, Annie had taken the decision out of his hands. If he and Annie couldn't find a way to work together after two months, then he'd pack it in. But if things worked out well, then he'd see if he enjoyed working at the auto shop as much as he had liked the law firm when he'd first started out. He wanted to do something that interested him, something that offered challenges and rewards.

He glanced up. Kevin stood staring at him with that same disbelieving look still plastered on his face.

"That's stupid, Tyler. You belong in Summerly. You know you do."

Tyler shrugged. "Maybe. Maybe not. But I'll probably be able to decide by the time eight weeks is up."

"And if you don't, are you just going to let Annie make up your mind for you?"

He knew Kevin would have a fit if he answered yes, so he hedged. "I might."

Before the other man could react, Karla announced over the intercom there was a phone call for Kevin, who tossed the clipboard he'd been using onto a box. "That's stupid," he repeated as he headed toward the door. "And the one thing you aren't is stupid."

There had been many times during the last few weeks when Tyler had felt very stupid, and confused, very confused. He sighed and leaned back in the chair. Maybe once he got his bearings and took on some responsibility, he'd feel better.

There was something else he needed to discuss with

Annie. They needed to discuss the attraction between them. The fire they shared all those years ago still burned, and they needed to decide what to do about it. He wasn't the only one feeling the chemistry. The attraction was so strong, he felt like he'd go crazy sometimes if he didn't hold her and feel the softness of her lips beneath his own.

Ultimately, he was every bit as drawn to her now as he'd been long ago. Life might have lost its spark for him during the last few months, but it hadn't left him for dead.

"Tyler, do you have a moment?"

Tyler glanced up to see Karla standing just inside the doorway. "Sure. What's up?"

She hesitated for a moment, and then slowly approached him. "I was wondering if you . . ."

The uncertainty in her voice made him worry that something was wrong. He stood and walked over to her. "Is there a problem?"

She laughed and shook her head. "No, I'm being silly." With a sigh, she looked up at him. "Here it is—will you go out with me?"

It took a moment for Tyler to realize she was asking him out on a date. She wasn't the first woman to ask him out, but considering how he felt about Annie, it wouldn't be fair to accept. Now the question was how to say no to Karla without hurting her feelings.

"I'd like to, really. But I'm involved with someone else."

She blinked. "You are? I didn't know you had a girlfriend. Annie never mentioned it when we talked."

"That's because Annie doesn't know." In fact, much to Tyler's disappointment, he was certain Annie was trying to deny that she felt the mutual chemistry between them.

He smiled at Karla. "I really am sorry, and I'm flattered you asked me."

Karla took the news with good grace. "That's okay. I understand. If you're already involved, then it's just my poor luck for asking too late."

"This woman and I go back a long time," he said. That was certainly true.

With a twinkle in her eyes, Karla nudged him. "Would your lady get jealous if we had lunch sometime? We could ask Kevin and Annie along to avoid any problems."

"Sure. Sounds great."

Annie wasn't the least surprised when Tyler appeared on her doorstep at a quarter to six. He hadn't listened to anything she'd said up to this point, so she hadn't expected him to listen now. She made no comment. Instead, she handed him Courtney, grabbed the baby bag, and locked the front door.

"I thought you'd be mad," he said as he walked with her to where his Porsche was parked.

Annie smiled and shook her head. "Not in the least.

Since that sports car of yours has no backseat, we have to take my car. If you want to drive over with us, that's fine."

Tyler stopped suddenly and turned to face her. "My car does too have a backseat. It's small, but she should fit."

"But her car seat won't. It's huge."

Rather than being upset, Tyler took the news in stride. "Okay, then you drive. I could use the rest."

Unable to stop herself, Annie laughed. "You really aren't going to have me drive you to your own house, are you?"

"Sure. And I'll have you drive me back here after dinner."

"That's ridiculous."

He cocked one eyebrow at her. "But safe. It will be dark by the time you and Courtney get back, and I want to know you got home without any problems."

Annie stared at him. He returned her look, more than a trace of fire lingering in his eyes. After a few seconds, he shifted Courtney onto his hip and moved until he stood next to Annie. She could smell the tang of his cologne and feel the warmth of his breath. Involuntarily, she nibbled on her bottom lip.

"I want to know you're all right," Tyler said.

Now what was she supposed to say to that? A lump formed in her throat at his words. His reasoning was silly and more than a little sexist. She didn't need Tyler Nelson to watch over her. Still, his softly spoken words made it impossible for her to say no. In fact, she seemed to find it impossible to say much of anything. Instead, she simply nodded and led the way to her car.

After Tyler buckled Courtney in her car seat, he settled in the passenger seat. Annie had never considered her sedan small, but it felt that way once Tyler was sitting next to her. To complicate the sensation, Tyler shifted to face her as she backed down the driveway. She felt his stare like a touch, and it unnerved her.

"Stop it, or I'll make you take your own car," she said without taking her eyes off her driving.

Tyler chuckled and didn't even pretend not to understand her. "You sure are grumpy these days, Annie. I don't remember you being that way."

Glancing briefly at him, she gave him a pointed look. "I guess you didn't know me very well."

"I guess I didn't."

His tone was wistful, but despite her curiosity, she refused to give into the need to glance at him. She already knew he looked wonderful. His hair was ruffled as if the wind had blown it, his jeans were worn just enough to mold his long frame, and his faded Harvard sweatshirt was shoved up on his forearms, revealing a tantalizing view of his tanned arms. Annie didn't even want to think about what she looked like. As usual, her makeup had long since worn off, and her blue dress was more functional than pretty.

"How's your mother feel about us coming?" Annie asked.

For a moment she thought he would comment on her obvious change of subject, but he didn't. Instead, he said, "She's thrilled, especially about seeing Courtney. I secretly think she's longing to become a grandmother."

That brought up an interesting point, and even though Annie knew she'd regret asking him this question, she couldn't stop herself. "So why haven't you married and had children?"

Tyler's good mood evaporated. "Touchy subject for us, don't you think?"

She glanced briefly at him. "I've been thinking about the past a lot, and I realize we were very young."

"Yeah, we were. And I'm sorry that I hurt you."

She hadn't noticed she was holding her breath until his words sunk in. "I know. So why didn't you marry after you got out of college?"

"At first I was too busy starting my career to get involved in anything but short-term relationships? Then I was too busy to have much time for relationships at all. I worked unbelievable hours."

The trace of bitterness in his voice made her look at him. She never thought Tyler would have regrets. He always seemed to know exactly what he wanted and exactly how to go about getting it.

"If practicing law means so much to you, why are you giving it all up to come back to Summerly?"

"Maybe I'm not. We'll have to see how the next eight weeks go."

They had arrived at his house, and since the gate was open, Annie pulled in and parked in front of the house. She shoved open her door and climbed out, anxious to put some space between them. Tyler retrieved Courtney from her car seat before Annie could, so she followed him up the walk. Her daughter giggled at the silly noises Tyler made, her delight in his company obvious.

"She's so wonderful," Tyler said over his shoulder.

Annie nodded. Yes, Courtney was great. Everything was great. Truthfully, she was less worried about Tyler's involvement than she was about them being able to grow the business correctly, so that they could compete. Business wasn't her specialty, and it certainly wasn't Kevin's. Her brother knew more about cars and trucks than any person Annie had ever met. But, unfortunately, he knew nothing about business. The Palmer family only knew how to run a small shop in a small town. They counted on the loyalty of their customers, who were also their neighbors. Over the last few years, though, Summerly had grown. New people were moving in; residents of long-standing were moving out. And new businesses, big businesses, were wooing away their customers.

Somewhere in the back of her mind, Annie had

known this was happening. She just hadn't wanted to face it. Glancing at Tyler as he opened the front door and held it for her, she was glad he'd forced her to face the truth.

"After you," he said, smiling down at her.

Annie tried to move past without brushing against him, but it proved impossible. With Courtney perched on his hip, Tyler took up most of the doorway. The only way to enter was to turn sideways and scoot by. When she was facing him, she glanced up, finding the grin she'd expected to see planted firmly on his face.

"You never grew up, did you?" she muttered.

He chuckled. "My philosophy has always been that when something works, don't change it."

Annie wanted to be mad at him, she really did. But it was difficult to stay angry with someone whose mere voice could send tingles dancing down her spine. It had been so long since she'd felt even a twinge of attraction to a man that a flirt like Tyler was difficult for her to handle. Talk about dancing too close to the fire.

With a sigh of relief, she made it past him into the foyer. For a moment, her surroundings distracted her from thinking about Tyler. It had been many years since she'd been inside the Nelson home. It had been lifetime ago. She'd only been invited to dinner once, and that evening had proven to be her last with Tyler. She hadn't slurped her soup or burped, or done anything at all to embarrass herself. But still, from the moment he'd figured out who she was, Tyler's father had made it clear that he didn't approve of the relationship.

On the way home, Tyler had apologized for his father's rudeness. When they reached her parents' house, he must have sensed how upset she was because he'd just held her and told her to forget his father. It didn't matter what Henry Nelson thought. All that mattered was how they felt about each other.

At that moment, settled in his arms, listening to his silken voice utter those soothing words, Annie had felt confident in their love. However, Tyler's father must have convinced him to call off the relationship, because two days later, he'd broken up with her.

She glanced over her shoulder at the man she'd once loved. Then she looked back at the living room. Everything had changed. The room looked different, and Annie felt different. There was no longer anything to fear.

"Don't think about the last time you were here," Tyler murmured from behind her. His hand rested lightly at her waist, but she didn't move away from him. She also didn't look at him, not wanting to see the kindness she sensed in his voice reflected in his eyes. Tyler being kind would be difficult for her to take.

Thankfully, Marguerite came in from the kitchen, a wide smile forming on her face the second she saw Annie and Courtney.

"I'm so glad you two could come to dinner. Dolores and I were just talking about how quiet this house is, and how much life a child would bring to it."

Annie choked on the laugh that threatened to escape. She'd never really known Tyler's mother. Up until the other night, Marguerite had struck Annie as a woman who'd been brought up to keep her own council. However, Tyler's mother had changed over the last few years and now obviously spoke her mind.

Marguerite walked over and smiled at Courtney. "How would you like to play in the backyard? We have a dog who loves children." She glanced at Annie. "Do you mind?"

Annie shook her head. "No, Courtney likes dogs." She moved forward, hoping to put some distance between herself and Tyler. Tyler solved her dilemma when he draped his arm around his mother's shoulders and, holding hands with Courtney, led the way to the large patio. Rather than a purebred dog as Annie'd expected, the dog Marguerite referred to was a friendly mutt who instinctively reacted gently to Courtney. After several admonishments, Annie finally got her daughter to stop kissing the "moddie."

When Marguerite took Courtney across the manicured lawn to play a game of fetch with the dog, Annie sank into one of the thickly cushioned lounge chairs.

"Courtney seems to like Pug," Tyler said, dropping on the chair next to her. "Why don't you get her a puppy?"

Turning her head, Annie studied him. He wasn't even looking at her, but she could feel his presence as strongly as if he were touching her. Absently, she rubbed her arms. "I have enough trouble taking care of Courtney without adding another creature to the formula."

Now Tyler did look at her. "Are you sure that's the reason? I'd hate to think you don't want the status quo to change, even by the tiny bit a dog would cause."

Surprised by his statement, Annie shook her head. "That's not true. I just don't want to take care of a dog."

Tyler studied her closely, his green gaze seeming to assess her in a way that made her uncomfortable. Finally, unable to stand the tension between them, she turned and watched her daughter instead. He was wrong. She didn't hate change, she just didn't like it, and she had every reason to feel that way.

"I know it's been tough, Annie."

Next to her, she heard the gentle scrape of the metal chair against the patio bricks as Tyler stood. She stiffened, expecting him to approach her. When she didn't feel his presence after a few moments, she glanced over her shoulder. He'd moved across the patio to the grill and was working on dinner. A strange feeling of disappointment engulfed her. Uncertain of the reaction she would get, she stood and slowly strolled over to join him.

"Can I help?" She deliberately kept her tone light.

The look Tyler gave her would melt ice in a blizzard. Annie sucked in a tight breath, uncertain of how to react.

"Things happen whether you want them to or not," he said.

Annie blinked, wanting to break the spell he cast around her. But it didn't help. His softly uttered words just increased her feelings of confusion.

"I know." Her voice was husky.

"We need to talk about what's happening between us."

Shaking her head, Annie backed away. Here in this house surrounded by memories of long ago was the last place she wanted to have this conversation. Truthfully, Annie wasn't sure she ever wanted to have it. Things were in enough upheaval. She wasn't ready to figure out how she felt about Tyler at the moment.

"Moddie run."

Annie spun around, grateful for the interruption her daughter provided. She picked up Courtney, knowing she was a coward to hide behind a small child. But she did it anyway.

And she kept doing it all evening. Courtney was always with her, either seated on her lap or straddling her hip. Her daughter's presence made it easy for Annie to avoid looking at Tyler. Her luck ran out, though, when he approached her after dinner ended.

"Do you want to go over my ideas for the business now?" he asked.

Annie couldn't think of anything she'd like less than to be alone with Tyler, but this discussion was the whole reason why she'd come over to his house in the first place.

She glanced at Marguerite. "Would you mind watching Courtney for a few minutes?"

Marguerite smiled and shook her head. "No, I'd love to."

Resigned, Annie headed toward the study, acutely aware of Tyler next to her. Some of her trepidation must have shown, because he chuckled when they reached the door.

"You know, I'm not going to cut off your head. You don't need to act as if you're going to your own funeral."

Annie walked inside and sat in one of the leather chairs facing the desk. She supposed she could argue with his assessment, but there really wasn't much point. Instead, she decided to ignore his comment and concentrate on the purpose of the meeting.

"So, what are these ideas?"

Tyler raised one eyebrow and gave her a questioning look. When she forced herself to maintain eye contact, he eventually sighed and sat behind the desk.

"Okay. We'll play this your way. I think for starters we need to expand, so we can match the lower prices of our competition. We also can share resources between several stores. That will keep us from being shorthanded when too many big jobs come into one store on the same day."

Annie kept herself from saying no immediately. She needed to keep an open mind about the changes, even if she personally didn't like the thought of changing a thing.

"How big of an expansion are you talking about?"

"I think we should add another store within the next couple of months. Then possibly a third store in the next twelve or eighteen months."

A knot the size of a grapefruit formed in Annie's throat at his words. She struggled to keep her anxiety under control. "You're kidding, aren't you? If we overextend like that, we could lose everything."

"No, we won't." Tyler leaned forward, his expression one of confidence. No wonder he was so good at persuading juries to go along with him. When he spoke, she was tempted to believe everything he said. He seemed so certain, almost as if he had his own personal view directly into the future.

But he could be wrong. It happened all the time to confident, successful people. They made mistakes like everyone else did. She certainly knew Tyler was capable of making a mistake, but rather than argue with him, she decided to take another approach.

"How do you intend to pay for this expansion? You've just bought Dad's share, and the initial outlay of cash will be a lot. It isn't cheap opening one of these stores."

"I'll supply the money."

Staring at him, Annie wasn't sure whether she'd lost her mind for listening to this plan, or whether he had for thinking it would work.

"Tyler, that's a lot of money. What if we're wrong? You could lose a fortune."

He shrugged casually, reminding Annie how little money meant to him. Tyler had always had money, so he probably thought he'd never be without it. For his sake, she had to talk some sense into him.

"You can't afford to lose that much money. No one can."

"I can always make more money," he said quietly.

Of course he could. He had another job to fall back on. "What does Kevin think about all this?" she asked once she had her feelings under control.

"He and I worked on some preliminary plans together, but we decided not to do anything until we ran everything by you."

"How thoughtful."

Tyler walked around the desk until he stood directly in front of her chair. Leaning back, he considered her for several silent moments. The tension in the air made her nervous, but she kept silent. Finally, he said, "Nothing will happen that you don't know about. And nothing will happen that you don't agree to."

His soft, deep voice made the words seem to carry a whole different meaning than just changes to the store. From the way her body reacted to that voice, he might have been talking about what would happen between them.

Looking at him, she felt the all-too-familiar coil of longing unfurl inside her. When he got that gleam in his eyes and looked at her like she was the only woman in the world, she had to fight the desire to melt into a puddle at his feet. Even knowing he was talking about the business didn't stop her breathing from becoming shallow and her fingers from tingling at the thought of touching him. For all she knew, he was using the attraction she felt for him to keep her off balance. She studied his face, looking for some sign of deceit in his deep green eyes. Instead, she found her own desire mirrored there.

Drat, why did this still happen to her, after all these years? Why couldn't they just sit in the room with each other without the persistent awareness surrounding them like a blanket?

"I'll think about what you said," she finally managed to say, although her voice was far from steady.

He moved toward her, one hand outstretched. "Annie, I really think—"

The door opened then, and Marguerite said, "Excuse me for interrupting, but Courtney's diaper needs to be changed, and I can't find the baby bag."

Annie turned toward the older woman. Marguerite had perfect timing. She used the distraction for all it was worth.

"I'll change her." Slipping from her chair, Annie

just barely managed to escape without brushing up against Tyler. When Marguerite tried to persuade her not to leave and just to say where the bag was, Annie insisted that they were through and she'd change Courtney.

If Tyler was disappointed by her behavior, he didn't show it. After changing her daughter, Annie found everyone sitting outside by the pool. Keeping a close eye on the adventurous toddler, she sat next to Marguerite. Throughout the rest of the evening, whenever she felt Tyler watching her, she'd duck her head and kiss the top of Courtney's blond head. By the end of the night, she knew he was becoming frustrated, but she didn't care.

Courtney had long since drifted off to sleep when Annie convinced Marguerite that she and Courtney needed to leave. Annie cradled the little girl's sleeping body close to her and snagged the baby bag on her way to the door.

"Wait a minute. I need to ride with you. My car's at your house."

At the sound of Tyler's voice, Annie stopped. Double drat, she'd forgotten about that. Glancing over her shoulder, she let her gaze finally rest on his handsome face. "Why don't you come by in the morning and get it?"

Not surprisingly, that crooked grin of his was almost her undoing. "I want to make certain you and

Courtney get home okay." He brushed a kiss on his mother's cheek. "I'll be back soon."

After Annie thanked Marguerite, she headed toward the front door. Tyler met her there and lifted Courtney from her arms. "This little girl sure gets heavy when she sleeps."

"Tell me about it." Annie followed him to her car, refusing to think about the ride home. She unlocked the back door and helped him secure Courtney in her car seat. Then she climbed in the driver's side and started the car.

"Are you going to be silent the whole way to your house?" Tyler asked once they were on the road.

"I'm tired."

Thankfully, they soon reached her driveway. Annie parked next to Tyler's Porsche and then climbed out of the car before they could resume the conversation. Without being asked, Tyler got Courtney out of the car and walked to the front porch with the sleeping girl cradled in his arms. Annie shifted her purse to the other shoulder, intending on taking Courtney from him, but Tyler moved the child out of her reach and shook his head.

"I'll take her in and put her to bed," he said.

A million things occurred to Annie to say, most notably that she didn't really need his help. Like most mothers, she was used to carrying her child. But the overhead lights on the porch let her see Tyler's face clearly, and she knew any argument on her part would be a waste of time. He had that determined male look she'd learned long ago only led to a useless discussion. The best way to handle this would be to get him out of her house as quickly as possible. Standing here in a circle of light surrounded by silent darkness was a situation bound to lead to trouble.

After unlocking the door, Annie pushed it open and then held it for Tyler as he shouldered his way inside and then headed down the hall to Courtney's room. The man had definitely spent too much time in her house lately.

"You should get an alarm system installed," Tyler said the second Annie appeared in the doorway to Courtney's room.

"I don't need an alarm," she said. Crossing to the dresser next to the crib, Annie took out a lightweight pajama set and then gingerly removed Courtney's jumper and T-shirt. Tyler leaned against the wall near the crib, but Annie kept her attention focused on changing Courtney. Why didn't he go home? Surely he was tired. She sure was; she felt like she hadn't slept for days.

Tyler didn't say anything else until she finished and settled her daughter down for the night. He followed her out of the bedroom and down the hall to the living room.

"I'd offer you something to drink, but all I have in

the house at the moment is apple juice, milk, and water."

Tyler stood in front of her, his hands on his hips. He looked frustrated, and he probably was. Tonight hadn't been a great evening for either one of them. They seemed out of sync on so many things.

"I don't want anything to drink. Annie, why do you have to be so stubborn about everything? You should have an alarm to protect yourself and your daughter."

Annie rubbed a tired hand across her forehead. "Look, if I put a mental bookmark at this point in the conversation, and I promise we can pick it up in the morning where we left off tonight, can we let it go?"

Tyler sighed. "Sometimes I feel like a man poking holes in his own life raft," he muttered.

Confused, Annie watched as he crossed the room to stand in front of her. Then, without comment, he leaned down and brushed his lips across hers. At first, she started to protest. She was confused about so many things. But then, the tingling sensation his caress evoked held her in place. She made no move to end the kiss, enjoying the sweet contact. Why did Tyler have this effect on her? He could turn her insides to jelly with just the lightest of kisses. He didn't even hold her in his arms. Instead, his hands remained by his sides.

Eventually, slowly, he raised his head, his gaze meeting and holding hers. Neither of them shattered the fragile silence surrounding them. But in that timeless moment, Annie felt as if their souls connected. And she knew she was teetering on the brink of falling for this man again.

Still without speaking, Tyler walked out the front door, closing it behind him. Standing in her darkened home, Annie fought conflicting feelings of desire and fear. What in the world was she going to do?

Chapter Seven

Despite his misgivings, Tyler found himself in a fragile truce with Annie during the next few weeks. Whenever he had a suggestion, she gave him the benefit of the doubt. . . . Well, after she first made him justify his opinion. But if he could back up his ideas with research, she would listen, and often agree.

"So you think this store is the right one?" Annie asked, wandering around the empty shop.

Tyler had found an empty auto repair building for rent across town. He'd done his research and put together a solid business plan. Now, standing in the six-bay shop, he knew in his heart it was the perfect location for their second store. Kevin had warmed to the idea immediately, but now he needed to convince Annie.

"You saw my proposal, and we've walked the building three times," he said, waiting until she faced him to continue. "Let's come at this from a new direction. . . . What don't you like about it?"

Kevin jumped in. "Opening this second store would be a change, and Annie hates changes."

Annie turned toward her brother. "That's not true." With a quick glance at Tyler, she added, "At least, not as much as I used to."

"But you still don't go after what you want in life; you still hide from it. Opportunity couldn't knock at your door because you've got a 'no soliciting' sign hung up."

"Cute. You sound like a twisted greeting card," Annie said.

Kevin gave her a pointed look. "Tell me I'm wrong."

"You're wrong."

Kevin snorted. "Tyler, tell me I'm wrong."

"You're wrong," Tyler said, and he meant it. "Annie's been open to suggestions for the last few weeks."

"She's hesitating now," Kevin said.

"Because this is a big decision." Tyler turned toward Annie. "I don't want to push you into agreeing to this store if you don't think it's a good idea."

She looked at him, her hazel gaze unwavering. "If we open this store, are you going to stay? Have you definitely decided not to go back to your law firm?"

Tyler's gut twisted into a hard knot. Truthfully, he

hadn't made a firm decision yet. There were so many things to consider. He hadn't enjoyed working at the firm for some time, but he'd poured years of his life into the place. He loved the law, or at least he did when the good guys won.

But he also loved Summerly. He loved seeing people he knew around town. He loved being part of Palmer Automotive and building something for the future.

He studied Annie's pretty face. Yes, there was a lot he loved about being home in Summerly. But would he stay? That was a different question. Annie deserved the truth, so he gave her the only truth he had at the moment.

"I don't have any plans to leave. I told my boss I wanted to take off for an unspecified amount of time, and that still stands."

Annie took a hesitant step toward him. "So you'll be here long enough to open this new store and get it going?"

Tyler swallowed past the lump in his throat. "Yes."

"So it's a deal, right?" Kevin asked his sister. "Tyler's agreed to stay, so you'll sign the lease on the store?"

"Okay," Annie said, her soft voice echoing slightly in the empty garage.

Tyler studied her, wondering if she'd ever truly trust him again. He could tell from her guarded expression that she'd agreed with some reluctance, probably hoping he wouldn't let her down. And he wouldn't, not like before. He wouldn't walk away from her and leave her in the lurch.

"Great." Tyler headed into what would become the waiting room. "I've got the lease contracts here. No time like the present to sign."

Glancing over his shoulder, he noticed Annie nibbling on her bottom lip. Seeing her worrying did funny things to Tyler's insides. "Things will work out," he assured her.

"Sure. They'll be great." She reinforced her words with a smile, but it was a weak one.

"Ah, Annie, like I keep saying, your only problem is you're bad with changes," Kevin said, leaning around Tyler to sign the contract.

"I already said yes." Annie moved forward and took the pen out of Kevin's hand. With deliberate care, she signed the contract, and then looked at her brother. "See, I just invited change into my life."

"That's a start. Now how about changing some more? How about going out on a date?" Kevin flashed a quick grin at Tyler. "I'm sure lots of guys would like to ask you out."

Tyler couldn't believe Kevin was doing this to his best friend and his sister. Matchmaking was a dangerous business at the best of times, but trying to put two old flames together was bound to end in disaster.

"Let's back off and leave Annie alone," Tyler said.

Annie's gaze never left her brother's face. "For your information, I have a date tonight."

Kevin's grin widened. "All right." He glanced at Tyler. "Way to—"

"Not with him. With Fred York. He's taking me to a party at his partner's house." Annie made the announcement with a smile, but it didn't last long when Kevin groaned. "What? Fred's a great guy. A terrific doctor."

"But he's not right for you, and you know it. You don't mind going on this date because you don't care how it turns out. You might as well take Courtney along, too. The date will definitely be a G-rated event."

This time, Annie groaned. "Kevin, drop it. You don't have a clue what you're talking about, and you're the last person to discuss relationships. You've only recently started dating women who are old enough to vote."

Tyler couldn't prevent a chuckle from escaping him. Annie had a point—Kevin's dates did tend to be young. Still, he'd almost forgotten about her planned date with the man Karla called Dr. Dreamy. He wasn't too happy about it, but what could he say? It wasn't any of his business.

Kevin was still fussing at his sister. "Fine. I'll back off, if that's what you want. But don't say I didn't warn you, and don't settle for boring and safe, Annie. You loved Paul. Find someone else to love. Someone who steams your glasses."

"I don't wear glasses." With a final pointed look at her brother, Annie turned to Tyler. "Are we done?"

Tyler nodded, pushing away the disturbing feelings that had overtaken him. "Yeah. We're done."

"Great. I need to head on home." Annie picked up her purse.

"To get ready for your date?" Tyler asked, and then felt like kicking himself when he did.

Annie turned toward him. "Yes." Then she left.

He watched her walk out, his emotions a tangled mess.

"Why don't you stop her?" Kevin said.

"Lots of reasons." Tyler stuffed the lease papers into his briefcase. He could feel Kevin watching him, so eventually, he gave in. "What do you want me to do? I'm not sure how I feel about your sister, okay? And I'm not going to mess with her head if I'm not."

"Fine. But it seems to me you won't know how you feel about her until you spend more time together."

"We already spend six days a week together."

"At work." Kevin smirked. "You need personal time together."

Tyler snapped his briefcase closed. "Yeah, well, she's dating someone else. I don't see the two of us getting together any time soon."

"I don't know about that. No doubt Mom is baby-sitting for Annie tonight. I could make a quick phone call. . . ."

Tyler stood still, rooted to the spot. He had so many

decisions to make in his life right now. Was it fair to get involved with Annie?

But then the image of Annie with another man twisted his gut, and his choice was made for him.

"Call your mom," Tyler said before common sense could change his mind.

She was going to make this date work, Annie decided as she studied the dresses in her closet. Fred was a wonderful man, a stable man, like Paul had been. Okay, so maybe Fred didn't rock her world, but he was a wonderful man, a man she could trust to be there when she needed him. Dr. Fred York was exactly what she needed.

Too bad she couldn't forget the way Tyler's kisses left her breathless. Or the way just a glance from him could kick up her pulse. But Tyler was the one who wasn't right for her. Just today, she could tell he was hedging when he'd promised to be there for the new store. The man hadn't made up his mind yet, and Annie wasn't about to let her heart get stomped on this time when he finally left Summerly.

And, unfortunately, Tyler would leave. She felt it in her heart. Tyler might think he was back for good, but she knew him. She knew how he thought. His mother would get better, and then Tyler would go back to his old life. He would never be happy living in Summerly.

No, at this point in her life, she needed someone

settled, someone she could depend on. No doubt about it, Fred was the right man for her.

"You're the baby-sitter?"

Tyler stood grinning at Annie, knowing there wasn't much she could do about the situation. Things couldn't have gone better. Annie's mom had quickly agreed to the change in plan. Now Tyler could check out this doctor and find out for himself what the man was like.

"Your mom can't make it," he said. "She asked me to fill in for her."

The door still blocked his view of everything except Annie's face, but he knew she wasn't ready for her date yet. Her hair hung in cute uncombed curls around her head, and her skin glowed with a recently scrubbed aura.

"Tyler, this isn't going to work," Annie said with a sigh.

Pushing lightly on the door, his grin grew when she released it and let him walk inside the house.

"I love Courtney," he said, trying to keep his voice even when he saw what she wore. She had on a faded red robe that was a little too short and a little too tight, and it made Tyler's blood pressure shoot up at an alarming rate. He cleared his throat. "Courtney loves me too." Needing to distract himself from the temptation Annie posed, he glanced around the living room. "So where is she?"

He didn't have to wait for an answer to his question.

Courtney peeked out from behind her mother's legs. The toddler let out a squeak of pleasure and ran to Tyler, her hands outstretched. "Man. Man."

Tyler scooped her up and gave her several noisy kisses, which reduced the little girl to a fit of giggles.

"Just look how happy Courtney is to see me," Tyler said, giving Courtney's pudgy cheek another loud kiss. "At least one of you Wylie women knows a great guy when she sees one."

He thought he heard Annie groan, but he wasn't certain. When he glanced at her, her attention was focused on the small gold watch on her wrist. After a few seconds, she nibbled on her pink lower lip, and he knew he had her.

"I guess I could call Kevin and ask if he could come over," Annie muttered, more to herself than to him.

"What's wrong with me?"

She looked at him, and he could see the confusion in her hazel eyes. "Why would you want to baby-sit? I'm sure you have better things to do."

He moved forward, so he could smell Annie's perfume. He'd formed an addiction to the sultry scent, which always sent his thoughts racing to what his life would be like if he had a caring wife and a precious daughter of his own.

Annie stood watching him through narrowed eyes. She still didn't trust him, but he knew he was eroding at her reservations like water on rock.

He smiled at her over Courtney's blond head. "Why

wouldn't I want to baby-sit? I'd like to help you. Plus I love this little girl."

For a moment, her gaze locked with his. Then, with a tiny shake of her head, she backed away from him, her fingers nervously playing with her watch.

"I don't have time to argue about this. Fred will be here any minute, and I'm not even dressed. Are you positive you want to do this?" she asked.

Tyler nodded, thrilled that she was relenting. "Yes, I'm sure. Now, what do I need to do for Courtney?"

With a sigh, Annie moved toward the hallway. Figuring she intended him to follow, he trailed behind her, admiring the view.

"I've fed her and given her a bath, but I didn't have time to read to her yet," Annie said without looking back at him.

"I know how to read. See how perfect I am for the job?"

Annie stopped suddenly. "I'm not sure this is such a good idea."

She still faced away from him, so he wasn't sure if she'd addressed her words to him or to herself. Deciding on the latter, he moved forward and rested his hand lightly on her shoulder.

"Don't worry about us. We'll be fine."

Not turning around, Annie simply nodded and walked into her bedroom. Once she shut her door, Tyler headed to Courtney's room. Whistling softly as he went, he decided coming tonight had been a good idea, a very good idea.

When the doorbell rang, he grinned at Courtney. "Let's go see what this Doctor Dreamy is like, okay?" Courtney babbled something, which he took as agreement, and he bounced her on his hip as he walked to the door.

He pulled it open with a flourish, enjoying the crestfallen expression on the doctor's face when he realized Annie wasn't in the doorway. Tall and thin with a face that struck Tyler as a little too pinched, the doctor underwhelmed him.

"Is Annie here?" Fred asked.

Reluctantly, Tyler shoved the door open to allow the other man inside. He didn't like the man, but it wouldn't do him any good to show how he felt. Years of dancing around the truth in a courtroom had taught him that sometimes the best way to win was to make the other side believe you'd lost.

"Yep. She's in the bedroom." He shifted Courtney, so he could extend his hand. "I'm Tyler Nelson. Annie and I are in business together."

His explanation of the relationship between Annie and himself seemed to take away some of Fred's suspicion. The doctor grasped Tyler's hand and shook it, the expression on his face changing from a frown to a smile.

"Oh, I thought for a second you might be an old boyfriend of Annie's."

Tyler desperately wanted to tell this man that he was, but now wasn't the time. It wouldn't win him any points with Annie if he made Fred mad. "I'm just helping out tonight by baby-sitting Courtney."

At the sound of her name, Courtney tipped her head and grinned up at Tyler. He tapped her nose, making her giggle. "Do you like kids?"

Fred nodded. "Yes, I do." He made no move toward Courtney.

The little girl didn't coo or babble at the dear doctor either. The toddler's complete attention was focused on Tyler, who rewarded her with another series of kisses on her plump cheeks.

"Hi, Fred. Sorry to keep you waiting," Annie said from the doorway.

Tyler turned at the sound of her voice and just barely managed to keep his mouth from dropping open. Annie had always been pretty, but tonight, she looked beautiful—no, more than beautiful—she looked . . . mesmerizing. Her knee-length black dress made her ivory skin seem so very touchable that it took all of his strength to keep from shoving the doctor out the door and keeping Annie to himself.

But he knew better than that. "You look great, Annie," he said, thankful that the attraction he felt at the moment didn't echo in his voice.

Still, Annie must have sensed his thoughts. Meeting his gaze, she looked at him for several long moments.

He only hoped she could read in his eyes what he longed to tell her.

"We really should get going," Fred said, breaking the spell that had settled around them.

With a nod, Annie pulled her gaze away and picked up her small black purse. "Are you sure you're okay with Courtney?"

Her soft voice made Tyler smile. She wasn't nearly as immune to him as she wanted him to believe. It wasn't the doctor who was making her heart race, and they both knew it.

"We'll be fine," Tyler said, taking the slip of paper Annie handed him with her cellular phone number written on it. Yep, he and Courtney would be just jim-dandy. But he was pretty certain Annie was in for a long, boring night.

"I had a wonderful time," Annie said, an overly bright smile glued firmly on her face. Actually, that wasn't true. She'd had a terrible time, but it wasn't Fred's fault. He'd been charming, and she hated herself for ruining the evening by calling every half hour or so to make certain Courtney was okay. Somewhere in the back of her mind, she suspected she'd called home less to check on Courtney and more to hear Tyler's voice. The look he'd given her right before she'd left had jangled her nerves, and she just wanted to get the evening over with.

"Is everything all right? You seemed distracted," Fred said.

Since Fred was only a few inches taller than herself, it was much easier for her to look up at him than it was to look up at Tyler. That was certainly something positive. She didn't have to almost break her neck to make eye contact. Now if she could only get her pulse to race whenever Fred came near her, she'd be all set. He was a nice man. A sincerely nice man who treated her with respect and didn't make her angry. He was everything a woman could want in a partner. In fact, he was downright perfect.

Annie sighed. Unfortunately, he wasn't the perfect man for her. She'd been lucky enough in her life to fall in love twice—once with that devil Tyler and then later with Paul. Falling in love with Tyler had been like going over Niagara Falls without even having a barrel for protection. Falling in love with Paul had been gentle and sweet, and she had truly loved her husband.

But she knew she would never feel love for Fred. Oh well, perhaps they could be friends, but the look on his face made her fairly sure friendship wasn't what he had in mind.

Maybe a kiss would help. Who knew? She might see skyrockets when he kissed her. It could happen. People fell in love all the time.

So when Fred slipped his arms around her waist and pulled her to him, she went willingly, hoping his kiss would prove irresistible. But as his lips brushed hers lightly, she knew with a tiny flicker of disappointment that it wasn't going to happen. All Tyler had to do was stand near her and her heart slammed in her chest, her stomach grew tight, and her skin tingled with anticipation. Once Tyler's lips touched hers, she felt like she was on fire.

Unfortunately, Fred's kiss was doing none of those things to her. The word *pleasant* floated through her brain with annoying repetition. Fred's kiss was pleasant.

Fred lifted his lips and rested his forehead against hers. "I had a great time, Annie."

She nodded. "Me too." Okay, so what did she do now? She didn't want to hurt him by launching into a let's-be-friends speech, but she also didn't want to lead him on. Before she could decide how to handle the situation, the porch light flicked on, and Tyler opened the front door.

"Hi, guys. How was the date?" He treated both of them to a lopsided grin that, as usual, made Annie's heart race.

Feeling a combination of relief and anger, Annie moved away from Fred. "Thanks for giving us a few minutes alone."

The sarcasm in her voice did nothing to dim the gleam in Tyler's smile. "Sorry to bust up the necking session, but it's late and I'd kinda like to head home."

Annie's anger evaporated. Of course he wanted to

go home. He'd been here all night. She moved toward the door. "You can leave now."

Tyler shook his head and pushed the door open wider, obviously wanting her to come inside. "I need to give you some messages and tell you about Courtney's evening." Turning to Fred, he added, "You don't mind, do you? I'm sure you have a busy day tomorrow too."

"Actually, I do." Fred brushed his fingers down Annie's arm. "I'll call you in the morning." With a nod at Tyler, he headed to his car.

Annie waved as Fred pulled out of the drive, not certain how she felt at the moment. She really didn't want to be alone with Tyler right now. It was too soon after she'd decided that Fred had no effect on her while Tyler made her pulse race.

Incredibly aware of the man standing in her living room, Annie moved toward the door, trying not to make eye contact with him and failing. His sparkling green gaze never left her face. Struggling to keep a grip on her shaky nerves, she brushed past him and walked inside. She went to Courtney's room and checked on her sleeping daughter, then returned to the living room.

"So tell me about tonight, and then you can head home." She deliberately tried to keep her tone light. "I'm not paying you enough to work overtime."

Tyler scratched his chin, his crooked grin still firmly on his face. "So, how was your date?"

Annie stiffened. "Okay. Courtney seems fine."

"She fell asleep about eight." Tyler took two steps toward Annie, his gaze never wavering from her face. "We had a terrific time. We played with her dolls, then read books." His voice dropped to a whisper as he moved closer. "Finally, we snooped through her mommy's stuff."

Annie was so caught up in the image of Tyler playing dolls with her daughter it took her a couple of seconds to grasp his words, but before she could get upset, she looked at him and realized he was teasing.

"Cute," she said. Still, she couldn't fault him when it came to Courtney. He was gentle with her little girl, which was a side of him she had never known existed until a few weeks ago.

He grinned again. "So how about you? Did you and the doctor hit it off?"

She tossed her purse on the couch. "We had a wonderful night."

"So why are you home so early? Isn't the party still going on?"

"Probably. But I was tired. Besides, I thought you said it was late. Don't you want to go home?" In fact, now she wanted him to go home. She wasn't really certain she could trust herself at this moment. She found Tyler Nelson way too appealing.

"In a minute." He moved until he stood directly in front of her. "So did I interrupt a great kiss? Is that why you're so mad? Was it as great as the one's we shared in my dad's Lincoln?"

Annie tipped her head so she could look at him. As much as she wanted to tell him to leave her alone, she knew she wouldn't. He was weaving his spell, seducing her with his gaze, with his words. She'd been so very lonely for such a long time, it felt wonderful to be alive again. Her blood soared through her veins; her heart slammed against her ribs. So many thoughts scrambled through her mind, images of the past, of her with Tyler, and of the kisses they'd shared.

She cleared her suddenly dry throat. "It was a great kiss," she lied.

He saw right through her. "No, it wasn't. If it had been, you'd be flushed and mussed and short of breath. But when I interrupted you two, you weren't any of those things."

"You're wrong. It was a good kiss."

Tyler chuckled, the deep rumbling sound making Annie's muscles tighten and her breathing become ragged. He ran one finger down the side of her face. "Come on," he murmured, bending his head toward her. "You and I both know there's a big difference between a good kiss and a great kiss."

She knew where this was headed, but she couldn't do a thing to stop it. His husky voice enticed her, lured her into playing his game, a game she definitely wanted to play.

"Maybe it was a great kiss," she said, her voice equally husky, her tone equally soft.

Tyler slipped his arms around her waist, and she

moved forward without any prompting on his part. "Well, was it a chaste peck like this?"

She did nothing to stop him when he dipped his head and placed his lips against hers. His light kiss was enough to make her legs feel shaky. She wanted him to deepen the kiss, but he didn't. Instead, he pulled away and studied her.

She shook her head. "No."

"Well was it a quick brush like this?" When his lips returned to hers, she slipped her hands over his shoulders and linked her arms around his neck. This time, the kiss was slower, longer but still, he ended the kiss much too soon for her liking.

"No." Her voice cracked as she answered him.

"How about a lingering good-bye," he said. When his lips met hers this time, he kissed her for several long minutes and then pulled back.

Annie couldn't prevent the quiet groan that escaped her lips. Tyler ran a string of soft kisses down the side of her neck. When his mouth returned to hers, he said against her lips, "Was the kiss a bone-melter, like this?"

"Um, no."

"So what kind of kiss was it?" he whispered.

"Tyler," she murmured, leaning against him. He made her feel safe and scared at the same time. "Don't make me fall in love with you again."

Tyler dropped his arms from around her and took a step back from her, a look of determination on his handsome face. "Would it be such a terrible thing if we fell in love again?"

Annie nodded slowly. "Yes. Because sooner or later, it would end. I don't want my heart broken again."

His sigh was heartfelt. "So you still don't trust me."

"I want to. I want to believe everything you say. But you aren't even willing to commit to a life in Summerly, so how can you commit to me? And I'd need a commitment, Tyler. I have to think about Courtney."

"I understand." Then, without waiting for her comment, Tyler dropped one final kiss on her mouth and walked to the front door.

"Good night, Annie," he said.

After he'd shut the door behind him, Annie sat staring at it, trying to figure out why she couldn't seem to get the happily-ever-after part of life right. Was wanting someone to love you and be there for you really so very much to ask?

Chapter Eight

Tyler had a headache by the time he got home from Annie's house. What in the world was he going to do? As he was kissing Annie, the realization had flooded through him that he loved her. This presented him with one huge problem. On one hand, he wanted her to love him back and share his life. He wanted to be a father to Courtney and a husband to Annie.

But on the other hand, he'd be giving up so much if he made that type of commitment to Annie. He'd automatically have to give up his position in the law firm. Annie was settled in Summerly and wouldn't want to leave, nor would it be fair to ask her.

So now he had to decide once and for all—did he stay in Summerly and commit to Palmer Automotive, or did he head on back to the firm? The decision was a tough one.

Still mulling over his choices, Tyler parked his car in the garage and headed across the yard to the back door. At times, being back home made him feel like a teenager again. The night's kissing match with Annie only compounded that feeling.

He smiled as he unlocked the door and slipped inside. The kitchen light was on, and he assumed his mother had left it on for him. Turning, he started to set the alarm when he spotted a note on the counter. It was from his mother. She'd gone somewhere with a friend and might be late coming home.

Glancing at the clock, Tyler frowned. It was almost midnight, much too late for a pair of elderly women to be driving around town, especially one who was just recovering from a major illness.

Tyler paced across the kitchen a few times, unsure of what to do. He'd never been the person doing the waiting before. With a niggling guilt, he realized his mother had always been that person. Many times when he'd been young, he'd tried to slip in the back door well after his agreed-to curfew. His mother had always been waiting for him. And every time, she'd kiss him and tell him how happy she was that he hadn't been hurt. Then she'd ground him for a week.

He'd been late the night Annie had first met his parents. After dropping Annie off, he'd driven around for a while, trying to decide what to say to his father.

When he thought he had a plan, he'd headed home and found his father waiting up for him.

Henry Nelson had been successful in business partly because he knew how to get what he wanted from people. He hadn't yelled or issued an ultimatum. He'd simply talked to Tyler about life and women and responsibility and sacrifice, about family loyalty and expectations, and a father's dreams and a mother's hopes, and finally, about what needed to be done.

The sound of tires on the gravel drive pulled Tyler's attention back to the present. He walked over to the door and looked out. A sedan he didn't recognize was parked halfway between the garage and the kitchen.

"Mom, it's too late to ask your girlfriend in," he muttered as he opened the door. He took one step outside and froze. The light from the kitchen illuminated the occupants just enough for him to see his mother lean across and kiss the man driving the car.

Tyler felt as if he'd been punched in the solar plexus. In a daze, he watched his mother push open her door and still laughing, climb out of the car. Before she shut the door, she leaned down and said something to the man. Tyler wasn't positive, but he thought he heard something about another date. Then she closed the door and waved as the man backed down the driveway.

"Hi, honey," Marguerite said as she walked toward her son.

A million things occurred to Tyler to say, but he

pushed them out of his mind. He kept a litany going in his head about his mother being a grown woman, and what right did he have to say anything about her dating? But underneath it all, Tyler was surprised and didn't know how to handle this situation. It wasn't that he thought she shouldn't date; she'd just never mentioned that she was.

"I didn't know you were seeing someone," Tyler said as she walked past him into the kitchen. All those years in a courtroom had taught him how to control his expression and his voice. His tone didn't sound accusatory, just interested.

His mother's expression was worried. "Are you upset?"

At her words, he realized he wasn't. In the back of his mind, he actually was happy to see her dating, for a lot of reasons. It meant she was feeling better. It meant she had her own life and interests.

It meant he could go back to his law practice without worrying about her.

"I'm just surprised you didn't mention it earlier," he admitted.

"I was afraid you'd get mad."

Now he felt like a heel. "Of course I wouldn't. You're a grown woman."

"I've known Carl for a long time, long before I got sick. But I asked him to wait until I felt better before coming to see me." She shot Tyler a quick glance. "In fact, I wasn't going to go with him tonight, but he tempted me with the promise of ice cream."

Tyler nodded slowly, unsure how he was supposed to act. This was one of those weird moments when a child feels like the parent. "How long have you been dating?"

"We aren't really dating. Not the way you think. We're more like friends."

You're friends who kissed goodnight, Tyler thought. "Why don't you have him over so I can meet him?"

His mother beamed at his words. She quickly crossed the room and hugged him. Tyler leaned down and kissed the top of her head, fighting the tightness in his chest. "The sooner the better, young lady. I want to know what sort of man you've taken up with."

Marguerite playfully shoved at her son's chest. "I guess fair is fair. I'll ask Carl over since I got to spend time with the person you're seeing."

Tyler's laugh was hollow. "I didn't have a date with Annie tonight, Mom. I watched Courtney while she went out on a date with another man."

The twinkle in his mother's eyes should have warned him. "Oh, really? Then why do you have lipstick on your cheek?"

Humming a little tune, she spun and headed up the back stairs, leaving her bemused son staring after her.

Tyler would never understand women, but he supposed it was better this way. If he understood them, he'd miss out on all the fun.

* * *

The more Annie thought about last night, the more she wished Tyler would decide to stay in Summerly—with Palmer Automotive—with her.

She no longer feared falling in love with him. She knew she'd already fallen. The question was what did she do about it?

Well, the first thing she planned to do was to bank the fire between them down to a simmer. So when Tyler came into her office at lunchtime, she greeted him with a polite smile. "How's your morning going?"

It gave her more than a little thrill that he looked as if his night hadn't gone much better than hers had. His hair was ruffled, and he seemed distracted. When he saw her, though, his expression brightened.

"Great." He moved several steps forward until he stood directly in front of her desk. "Care to join me for lunch today? I think we should talk."

That silky, deep voice of his made the invitation sound like a promise of heaven. He was right; they needed to talk. "Okay."

She pulled her purse out of her desk and crossed the room to join him by the door. As she got close to him, her heart began the same erratic rhythm she'd come to associate with being around Tyler. It was increasingly difficult to stand this close to him and not want to kiss him. Good gracious, how was she going to simmer this relationship down if she couldn't even spend a few normal minutes with the man?

Tyler shifted so she could precede him, and she couldn't help but notice he'd left enough room so she wouldn't brush against him. That was a smart move. After telling Kevin where they were headed, they walked to Tyler's car. Silence hung awkwardly between them. Annie glanced briefly at her black pumps, hoping lunch wouldn't lead to another verbal battle between the two of them. Tyler had spent the last few years learning how to win any argument, while she hadn't even been on the debating team in high school. It was like taking on a sharpshooter with a gun filled with blanks.

But life with Courtney had taught Annie a few things, not the least of which was to stand your ground even if it was a bit shaky.

She was thankful that Tyler chose a restaurant close to the store. They made polite chitchat on the drive, and then once they were settled in the booth, Tyler leaned back against his seat.

"About last night," he said. "I need you to know I didn't plan that kissing session."

"I know." She shifted the silverware in front of her. Before she had to say anything else, the waitress appeared to take their order. Once the woman left, Annie glanced back at Tyler. There was no time like the present to have an honest discussion. The restaurant was practically empty, so no one would overhear them.

"Look, Tyler, I can't deny I'm attracted to you. I've always been." She drew a deep breath into her lungs, gathering her courage to tell him how she felt. As she looked into his blue eyes, words escaped her.

"Things do seem to be getting pretty serious between us," he supplied.

"Yes. They do." She leaned forward, needing him to understand how she felt. "But as I said last night, I have to think about Courtney."

Anxiously, she waited for Tyler's response. Finally, he sighed. "I know."

When he didn't say anything else, disappointment filled her. "Then we understand each other."

He reached across the table and covered her hand with his. Briefly, he glanced away, and when his gaze returned to her face, his expression was serious. "I've fallen in love with you again."

Annie pulled her hand away, surprise and joy rushing through her. "You're kidding, right?"

" 'Fraid not." He studied her face and then added, "It's not the end of the world, Annie. If you don't feel the same way, just say so. I'll back off. But I wanted you to know how I felt."

Tears burned her eyes. Why did he have to say this now? "How can you be in love with me? You're not even sure you're going to stay in Summerly."

Tyler chuckled softly. "One doesn't have anything to do with the other, sweetheart. I can love you without deciding to stay here."

"So even being in love with me, you might leave? What about your mother? Doesn't she need you?"

"Apparently not. She's feeling well enough to start dating someone."

Annie felt as if her entire world had spun out of control. Tyler loved her, but he still might leave her. She wanted to tell him that she loved him too, but what good would that do? He'd just said he might leave.

He blew out a loud breath. "Any chance you're in love with me too?"

She looked at him, her pulse beating frantically. "I don't know. Maybe." Glancing up at him, she admitted, "Probably."

A slow grin crossed Tyler's face. He leaned forward and opened his mouth to say something when his cellular phone rang. Still watching Annie, he removed the phone and answered. Annie turned her attention to the window, but when Tyler's voice became tense, she looked back at him. His face was pale as he handed her the phone.

"It's Kevin," he said. "Courtney—"

"What's wrong?" Annie demanded, fear rising in her throat. This couldn't be happening. Nothing could be wrong with her precious daughter.

"Courtney had a seizure at day care. They've taken her to the hospital," Kevin said.

That was all Annie needed to hear. She jumped to her feet, grabbed her purse, and bolted to the door. It was only after she'd reached the car that she realized Tyler was right beside her. He unlocked the car, and they both silently climbed inside. On the ride to the hospital, he held her hand. Annie found the wordless contact oddly comforting.

Annie hit the door to the emergency room at a sprint. The nurse on duty directed her to the small cubicle where Courtney lay on a table as Ginny from the day care center held her hand. When Annie saw her still and silent daughter, a sob escaped her.

"Sweetheart, it's Mommy. I'm here," she said, kissing her daughter's face. Courtney mumbled and continued to sleep. Frantically, Annie looked around. A woman stepped forward.

"I'm Doctor James. Your daughter has spiked a high fever, and that caused her to have a febrile seizure."

Annie struggled to understand what the doctor was saying. "What caused the fever?"

"She has an ear infection, which we're treating, and her fever has dropped. She's going to be fine."

Relief overcame Annie, and she didn't realize she was shaking until she felt a strong arm slide around her waist. Glancing up, she looked into Tyler's concerned face. He smiled gently at her and brushed her cheek. With surprise, she realized he'd wiped tears from her face.

"Can we take her home?" Tyler asked.

The doctor nodded. "I'll release her in about an hour if she continues to improve. Call your pediatrician if you have any further problems."

Annie leaned over and kissed Courtney, thrilled that she would be fine. "I love you, Pea Pod." Then, she glanced at Tyler. She could see the same love for the child echoed in his face. He loved her daughter too. He loved them both.

She moved into his arms and let him hug her.

"Everything's going to be fine," he murmured to her.

Annie nodded, hoping he was telling the truth.

Three days later, Tyler stood on the front step of Annie's house and rang the doorbell. She was probably going to tell him to take a hike, but he'd been sent on a mission from her mother, so he had a job to do.

Slowly, Annie opened the door. She looked exhausted, and Tyler's heart went out to her.

"Hi, Tyler. You know, you don't have to stop by all the time to check on Courtney." Annie yawned. "She seems fine today."

Tyler gently moved Annie away from the doorway and glanced around the living room. When Courtney saw him, she ran over and he scooped her into his arms.

"Hi there, peach cheeks." He gave her a kiss since he was so thrilled that the little girl was feeling well again. She'd been steadily improving over the last few days, and now she positively beamed. "Want to visit Grandma?"

Annie blinked at him. "Grandma? What are you—"

Tyler leaned forward and dropped a quick kiss on Annie's forehead. "Your mother asked me to bring Courtney over for the day. We all agree you've exhausted yourself, so your mother wants to keep Courtney until tomorrow morning, so you'll get some rest."

"But Courtney needs me," Annie said softly.

Tyler shook his head. "No, she's fine. Right now, you're the one who needs care. You've gotten very little sleep during the past few days. You need to rest before you get sick."

When Annie opened her mouth to disagree, Tyler bent his head and kissed her, silencing any argument she might have. He felt the impact of that kiss clear to his toes. How he loved this woman. With great reluctance, he pulled away.

"Courtney, do you want to visit Grandma?" Annie asked, her gaze never leaving Tyler's face.

"Mame," Courtney said with a giggle. When Tyler put her on the ground, the little girl hurried to her bedroom.

"Guess she's gone to pack," he said as he trailed after her. Between the three of them, they managed to gather Courtney's belongings, then Tyler headed toward his car. In the doorway, he couldn't prevent himself from dropping another kiss on Annie's soft mouth.

"I'll see you later," he said, knowing he would. "You sleep."

This time, Annie didn't argue with him. She simply nodded and waved good-bye.

Annie was expecting Tyler to stop by after work. After sleeping all day, she felt like a million dollars. When she woke, she called her parents' house to check on her daughter, then showered and put on her prettiest dress. It was made for summer, with a tiny flowered pattern and a full skirt that was long and flowing. She took extra care with her hair and makeup, wanting to look wonderful.

Her efforts were rewarded by the stunned expression on Tyler's face when she opened the front door. Annie didn't need any flattering words to know he thought she looked great. Still, she got them.

"Wow, Annie. You look . . . wonderful."

"Thank you." She started to move out of the doorway to let him come inside, but he shook his head.

"I have dinner reservations for us," he said, taking her hand in his and tugging her outside.

Annie laughed, loving this fun side of Tyler. "I'm not dressed for anyplace fancy."

Tyler headed toward his car. "This place isn't fancy. Just special."

And it was. Tyler took her for a picnic by the lake outside of town. As they ate cold fried chicken, they watched the sun set. Neither of them brought up the past. Instead, they talked about Courtney and the business.

When it became too dark for comfort, they packed his Porsche and headed back toward town. As they neared her house, Tyler said, "You know, we never got a chance to talk about our shared confessions the other day."

Annie didn't pretend not to know what he meant. "Are you sincerely in love with me?"

"Yes."

"Enough to build a life with me here in Summerly?" she whispered, her love for him swirling inside her.

Silence settled in the car. After parking in her driveway, Tyler got out and walked around to open her door. The suspense was killing Annie, but she knew she needed to let him answer in his own time. When they reached her porch, he leaned against the front door and studied her.

"I love you too much to lose you again. So, yes, I love you enough to stay in Summerly with you."

Happiness washed through Annie. Smiling, she came toward him, stopping when he gathered her into his arms. "I love you too," she said. Then she kissed him deeply. She felt his love in his kiss and in the tender way he held her. Maybe things really would work out for them. Maybe they could truly find happily-ever-after.

She certainly hoped so. Because she knew now, if he left her again, the heartbreak would be more than she could take.

* * *

Tyler's life had never been better, he decided two weeks later. After that miraculous night when he'd promised to stay in Summerly with Annie, they'd spent their days together at the shop and their evenings together at her house. He was one happy guy.

He glanced at his watch. It was too early to ask Annie to lunch, but maybe he could stop by her office and coax a quick kiss out of her. Before he could stand, the phone on his desk rang. Tyler answered it, and immediately wished he hadn't. Bernie Savan, senior partner at the law firm and Tyler's boss, was on the line.

"Tyler, glad I found you. Your mother said you were at this number. Look, I know I agreed to your extended leave, but things have changed. The Collins case is in jeopardy. I fired Carl Matherly. I need you to come back and take over."

Tyler felt as if a vise tightened around his heart. Bernie Savan had been his father's best friend. He'd given Tyler a great job fresh out of college, and he owed the older man. But his life was different now.

"I can't come back, Bernie. In fact, I've been meaning to call you. I've decided to leave the firm. I'm moving back to Summerly permanently."

"You can't, son. The firm needs you. *I* need you. If we lose this case, we can kiss a large part of our revenue good-bye." His tone dropped, and Tyler realized with a start that suddenly his friend sounded old. "I'm retiring soon. I can't lose everything at this point.

Can't you do it for old time's sake? I won't need your help for long. Six months. Maybe a year. Then you can leave."

Pain shot through Tyler. He hated to disappoint Bernie, but how could he explain this to Annie? The Collins case was huge. Spending a year was likely if he returned. He'd have to put in impossible hours. There'd be no time for visits to Summerly. In fact, he'd have no time for anything.

And the new store was due to open next week. Annie would never forgive him if he left now.

"Bernie, I can't. I just—"

"Tyler, I hate to do this. You know I love you like a son. But I did help you when times were tough. Now I need you to return the favor."

Tyler closed his eyes and leaned back in his chair. Bernie was pulling out all the stops. Right after Tyler's father had died, Bernie had helped pay off some large debts Henry had accumulated during his last years. They were debts a struggling law student couldn't pay, and Tyler's mother hadn't known what to do.

Bernie had stepped in, paid the debts, then hired Tyler. Over the years, Tyler had more than paid the older man back. But he owed Bernie more than money. The man had been there for the Nelson family when they'd needed help. There was no way Tyler could refuse to help him now. Even if it meant that Annie wouldn't understand, he had to say yes. And it was killing him.

"Okay, Bernie. I'll help," Tyler said, feeling like he'd just sealed his own fate.

Annie glanced up when Tyler entered her office. She started to smile, but something in his manner stopped her. When he shut her office door, she knew something was wrong.

"What's the matter?" she asked, half fearing she already knew the answer.

"I just got a call from Bernie Savan."

Annie felt her heart drop to her toes. "Your boss at the law firm?"

Tyler nodded. "Annie, I don't know how to tell you this. I need you to know that I love you. I love Courtney. I would never—"

"You're leaving, aren't you?" She blinked against the sudden tears in her eyes. How could she have been so stupid a second time?

He dropped into the chair across the desk from her. She could see the pain on his face, but it didn't help. He was going to leave again.

"Bernie has an emergency at the office. I need to go help him."

Annie nodded, struggling to hold in the tears. "I see."

Tyler leaned forward. "No, you don't. I owe this man, Annie. I can't let him down. You wouldn't love me if I was the type of man to turn his back on a friend."

"And I do love you, Tyler." She drew a shaky breath into her too-tight lungs. What would Courtney think when Tyler stopped coming over? Would her daughter miss him the way Annie knew she would miss him? But maybe it wasn't as bad as she feared. Maybe he wasn't leaving forever.

At her declaration of love, Tyler circled the desk to stand next to her chair. He knelt and took her hands in his. "This hurts me too. But I have to go."

"How long will you be gone?"

When he paused, she knew the answer was bad.

"At least six months. Probably longer," he said.

Annie felt a tear slip free. "I see. Will you be able to come back on the weekends?"

"No." He took her hands in his, his gaze locked with hers. "Come with me. Marry me, and come with me."

She slowly shook her head, despair overwhelming her. "I can't. My life is here. Courtney's life is here. I have plans, commitments. We both can't leave Kevin to run things by himself."

"Annie, please, you have to come with me. I love you. I need you with me."

She felt another tear slip free. "I can't. We want different things from life."

"No, we don't. I want you. I want Courtney. I want to live here with you."

"Then don't leave." She knew she was being unfair, but she couldn't help it. She didn't want him to leave, not now, not when she'd finally found love again.

"I have to. I owe this man."

But you love me! she wanted to scream. Still, she knew this was hurting him as much as it hurt her.

"What about the stores? Kevin and I can't afford to buy you out right now."

"I don't want my money back." He leaned forward and brushed a kiss on her cheek. "We don't have to end here. We can find a way around this."

Slowly, she shook her head. There was no reason to pretend. He'd go back to his law firm, and six months from now, he'd be caught up in his old life.

"No. It's better to end things," she said. "You need to go back to where you belong. I need to get on with my life here. It was fun while it lasted."

Tyler stood. His expression showed how much her words hurt him. But he didn't argue. Instead, he walked to the door. After he opened it, he turned to face her. "Don't you wish just once things would work out for us?" he asked softly. Then he walked out.

Chapter Nine

Tyler glanced at the clock on his desk: 3:00 in the morning. He might as well admit it—he wasn't going back to his apartment tonight. Rubbing a tired hand across his eyes, he stood and crossed over to the leather sofa in the far corner. Flopping down, he closed his eyes and tried to think about anything but Annie.

Unfortunately, his brain wouldn't cooperate. Memories of Annie haunted his days and filled his dreams at night. He missed her so much it hurt. He missed her smile, her warmth, everything about her. He also missed Courtney. The little girl had worked her way into his heart.

Thanks to the pace he'd kept up during the last few days, he was exhausted. Ever since he'd returned to the firm, he'd put in incredible hours. Bernie hadn't been kidding when he'd said the case was a mess. The firm would be lucky if it didn't lose, and a loss in a high-profile case like this could cost them big bucks. Other clients would start to have doubts when they read about the problems in the paper. And new clients would be reluctant to hire a firm that had lost such an important case.

So it was up to him to make certain they didn't lose. Bernie was counting on him. Tyler groaned and rubbed his temples. But what about Annie, and Courtney, and Kevin? Hadn't they been counting on him too? Hadn't Annie and Kevin rented the new store thinking he'd be around to help the business grow? Yet here he was, in the middle of the night, hundreds of miles away. Once again, he'd let down the woman he loved.

And it was driving him crazy. In two days, Palmer Automotive's new store would open—without him there. Knowing sleep was out of the question, Tyler sat up and leaned his head in his hands. This couldn't keep up. He couldn't put in these kinds of hours and then not sleep at all. He'd lose his mind, if he hadn't already. There had to be a solution somewhere. Surely he could think of something if he thought hard enough.

Heading over to his desk, he grabbed a legal pad and pen. Returning to the couch, he jotted down some ideas. First, he needed to make certain the firm didn't lose this case. Second, and equally important, he needed to find a way to be there for Annie and Kevin. So how could he be in two places at the same time? The obvious answer was that he couldn't be. But he wasn't settling for the obvious. Without stopping to think, he wrote down every possible solution that came to mind, even the ridiculous ones. Finally, he had almost a page of ideas.

"Somewhere on this page is the solution to my problem," he muttered to himself. And he would find it; he had to find it because once he did, he could return to Summerly and the woman he loved.

"So how's everything shaping up?" Kevin asked as he entered the new store.

Annie watched her brother walk across the waiting room. He looked as tense as she felt. This new store made both of them nervous. What if they couldn't pull it off? What if they lost everything by overextending?

"I think all the details are set, and with a couple of days to spare. I keep worrying that there's something I forgot, but I can't imagine what it would be." She stood and brushed her hands on the sides of her jeans. After Tyler left, she'd taken over responsibility for the new store. Staying busy helped her think of things other than Tyler . . . and her broken heart.

"Seems like you've got it all covered," Kevin said, coming over to stand next to her. "Looks great."

Something in his attitude caught Annie's attention.

This was more than simple nerves. He had something on his mind, something serious.

"What's wrong?" she asked.

Kevin shrugged. "Nothing really. I guess I can't help wishing Tyler could be here for the opening tomorrow."

"Kevin, look—"

He held up one hand. "I know. He's busy. But he did call me last week to check on the store . . . and other things. I thought since he was still interested, he might stop by."

Annie hated to disillusion her brother, but he obviously didn't know Tyler very well. The man had left, just like that. He'd made his choice, and he'd chosen his law firm. It was that simple.

"Don't let it bother you," she said, wishing she could heed her own words. "At least he's still giving us funding." That was the reason she'd been able to get everything done quickly. She'd had enough capital to do things correctly and didn't have to scrimp on equipment.

Absently, Kevin nodded, and Annie knew he wasn't really listening to her. He missed Tyler. In the short time he'd been in Summerly this time, Tyler had managed to work his way into the hearts of Annie's entire family. She'd lost a love, and Kevin had lost a friend.

"How're you holding up?" Kevin asked, turning to look at her.

"Fine." She stuffed her hands in the front pockets of her jeans.

"Don't you miss him?"

Does the sun set in the west? But she didn't say that to Kevin. Instead, she told him the truth. "Yes."

"So why didn't you go with him?"

Stunned, Annie stared at Kevin. "Go with him? Why would I go with—"

"Because you love him," Kevin interrupted. "Because you've always loved him."

"I . . ." She turned to walk away, wanting to end this conversation before she did something silly and started to cry, but her brother stopped her with a gentle hand on her arm.

"Annie, I may not be the smartest guy in the world, but anyone can see you love Tyler. Before he left, you were so happy, and the two of you are great together. So why'd you stick around? Why didn't you follow him to New York? Didn't he ask you?"

With difficulty, she swallowed past the large lump in her throat. "Yes, he asked me, but I said no."

"Why'd you do that?"

Annie blinked, annoyed to find tears filling her eyes. "Because my life is here. Courtney's life is here. I can't just drop everything and follow Tyler to New York. Even if I did, I'd hardly get to see him there. He said he'd always be working."

Kevin dropped his arm around her shoulder. "But

at least you'd get to see him some, which is better than what you've got now."

Her heart constricted at his words. "Yes." Her voice was a mere whisper. "Yes, it would be better."

"Then why stay here? Go be with him."

Annie moved away from Kevin. "Because what kind of life is that for Courtney and me? Stuck in a strange city with no friends or family, hoping Tyler will come home from the office and spend a few minutes with us?"

"I guess I don't see it that way. I've never been lucky in love like you are, but if I was, it seems to me I'd give about anything to spend at least some time with the person I loved." He studied her, his eyes narrowed. "Unless this is about more than just Tyler working so many hours. Is this about me and the stores? Tell me you're not sticking around for me."

"No. Not just for that."

He latched onto the uncertainty in her voice. "But it is some of what's keeping you back, right?"

She knew where he was headed with this. "Okay, I'll admit part of the reason I'm staying is because of the stores. Of course I am. My livelihood depends on Palmer Automotive. I'm not going to walk away and leave you to run it all by yourself, especially now that we're opening a new store. You're not superhuman. You can't run both stores by yourself."

Kevin rubbed his thumb across his chin, a gesture

Annie knew meant he was thinking about what she'd said. "You're probably right."

"I definitely am."

"But I could hire some help." He smiled. "I could hire a few managers who could—"

"Bankrupt us in a few months," Annie tossed out. "You have a new store to run. You can't afford any unnecessary expenses."

"But we're not paying Tyler's salary. That enables me to hire some people."

Annie bit her bottom lip, debating what to do. She wanted to find a way, any way, to be with Tyler. Maybe she could go after they got this store up and running. Maybe they could hire a manager, especially if Annie didn't draw a salary either. Tyler had asked her to marry him. She could do that. She could marry him and live with him in New York. Since she wouldn't have to work, she could spend her days with Courtney. That would be a real plus. Naturally, they would continue to give Kevin financial support if the new store needed it.

The idea started to take form in her mind. As Kevin had pointed out, even though she might not see him a lot over the next few weeks, she would at least see him sometimes. Which would be better than what she had now—which was nothing.

"I don't know," she admitted softly. "I'd like to, but—"

"You think it wouldn't be fair, right?"

Annie nodded and studied her brother's face. "I know it wouldn't be fair."

Kevin chuckled. "Yeah. Instead of always bumping heads with you, I'd have a manager who would have to do what I wanted. I can see how that would be a real downer."

Annie smiled, and her smile grew into a grin when Kevin hugged her.

"Go to New York and be with Tyler. If I run into any problems, I'll call."

"But I'm not leaving until after the opening tomorrow."

Kevin shrugged. "Whatever works for you. As long as you go."

Annie felt like a weight had been lifted from her shoulders. She really could do this. She could make this change in her life and spend her days with her daughter and her nights with Tyler. Suddenly the world seemed full of possibilities. Paul's death had shown her how easy it was to lose someone you loved. And she did love Tyler, with all her heart. She knew how lucky she was to find that kind of love again in her life.

And she wasn't going to throw his love away.

"Bernie, I need to talk to you." Tyler walked into his boss's office and dropped into a chair. "I'm not having any fun."

With a chuckle, Bernie switched off his computer

and gave Tyler his complete attention. "Son, this is the law. No one ever said it would be fun."

"I know. But the thing is, I used to think practicing law was fun. I liked everything about it. But I don't anymore."

The smile on Bernie's face faded. "This is about you going home, right? I thought you understood how serious this case is. I can't afford to lose it."

Tyler nodded and drew in a deep breath. Then he launched into his plan.

"I don't want to stay. I'll admit that. I'll also admit I realize how important this case is. For that reason, I've done a lot of thinking about other ways we could handle this. For starters, you need to replace me."

Bernie made a croaking noise. "No way. Where would I find another lawyer as good as you are? I've spent years teaching you to be great."

Tyler smiled. "I know. And I appreciate it, Bernie, I really do. But my life isn't here anymore. I want to go back to Summerly."

"What's so special about that place?"

"It isn't the place. It's the people. I left behind . . . someone I love very deeply." Images of Annie flashed through Tyler's mind. Soon he'd be back in Summerly. Maybe then she'd forgive him for leaving in the first place. Maybe then he could talk her into marrying him.

"I can't make it without you," Bernie said.

"Sure you can. I've called a couple of the hotshots

I went to law school with. You're one lucky son of a gun. Margaret Donnelly will consider joining the firm if you put together the right sort of package."

At the mention of Donnelly's name, Bernie leaned forward. "I've heard of her. She's good."

Tyler's heart rate increased. This might just work after all. "Very good. And I can have her up and running in no time. Besides, if she has any questions, she can call me. But I will need tomorrow off."

He could tell from Bernie's distracted expression that the older man was already making plans. Tyler's excitement grew.

"Okay, I'll go along with it," Bernie said finally. "I know how much it means to you to go back home. I can't help saying I think you're giving up a lot. I hope that woman is worth it."

Tyler grinned. "Oh, yeah. She's worth it. She's more than worth it."

Annie glanced out into the waiting room. It was packed. It had been packed all morning, thank goodness, which was a good sign. She'd been worried that their reputation hadn't spread across town, but obviously it had.

"We're officially a hit," Kevin said, entering the small office Annie had been temporarily using while she oversaw work on the store.

"It does seem to be going well."

"We've got more work than we can handle. I've

also got a lead on a manager. Things here look terrific." He nudged her. "So why haven't you left? Don't you have a plane to catch?"

Bemused, Annie shook her head. "No. I'm going to wait a few days to see—"

"Hi, sweetheart." Annie's mother appeared in the doorway. "We thought you'd be gone by now."

Annie looked from Kevin to her mother and then back again. "What are you guys up to? I'm not leaving. I haven't even booked a flight yet. Plus, I need to make arrangements for Courtney. Mom, in fact, I planned on calling you later today. Could you please watch—"

"Man. Man." Courtney popped her head through the doorway, looked around, and then asked her mother, "Man? Man?"

"She's looking all over the place for Tyler," Annie's father said, negotiating his way through the crowd and sitting in the chair in front of Annie's desk. He looked at her and grinned. "What are you still doing here?"

Love for these wonderful people filled Annie's heart, and she blinked away a quick tear. She would have to come back for regular visits because she would miss her family too much to stay away for long.

"What are you and Mom doing here?" she asked, giving both of her parents a hug and picking up Courtney.

"Well, we stopped by to say good-bye before you head to New York." Her dad winked at her mother.

"And since we'll be keeping an eye on Courtney for the next couple of days, we thought you probably would want to give her a kiss good-bye."

Annie smiled at her parents and brother over the top of her daughter's head. "Does this mean I'm free to head off to New York?"

Kevin dropped an arm around her shoulders. "Actually, it means more than that." He reached into his back pocket and pulled out an airplane ticket. "It means that you've got just enough time to hurry home and pack a suitcase. Your flight leaves in a few hours."

He handed Annie the ticket, and she studied it with wonder. "You guys are the best."

"Have you told Tyler you're coming yet?"

Annie shook her head. "No. I'm going to surprise him." She didn't add that she hoped Tyler found it a good surprise. She didn't want to think about the possibility that he'd changed his mind.

"We'll see you after you work out all the details with Tyler." Her mother kissed her forehead. "I'm happy for you, sweetheart."

Annie hugged her in return. "I'm pretty happy myself." She glanced at Kevin. "Are you certain I don't need to stay?"

Kevin shook his head. "Positive. Now hurry on home and pack your suitcases. We paid a lot for that ticket, and it's nonrefundable."

"Thank you," she whispered and dropped a kiss on his cheek. "I really appreciate this."

Kevin winked at her. "I know."

With a final group of hugs, she headed to her car. She was starting to believe things were going to work out after all.

Tyler couldn't remember the last time he'd been so nervous. He'd never been this upset even when facing a really tough jury. But he knew why he was so worried—this meant more to him. Annie might tell him to buzz off, and if she did, he had no idea what he'd do. He loved her too much and couldn't imagine his life without her. No, today was the most important day in his life so far, and he didn't want to blow it.

That was why it took him so long to walk from his car to her front door. He'd already stopped by the new shop looking for her. Kevin had laughed when he'd seen him and told him Annie was at home but he hadn't said why. Tyler couldn't imagine her not being at the new store on opening day. He just hoped she wasn't sick.

With his heart in his throat, he rang the doorbell and waited impatiently. Seconds seemed like hours while he waited. When Annie finally opened the door, she stared at him for a moment. Her eyes widened, then with a squeal, she launched herself at him and wrapped him in a tight embrace. Before Tyler could say a single word, she kissed him hard enough to curl his toes.

When she finally released him, joy flooded through

him and he smiled down at her. "This is a much better welcome than I'd hoped for." At her urging, he followed her inside and shut the door behind him. "The reason I'm here is because I want to ask you to forgive me."

Annie blinked at him. "Forgive you for what?"

"For leaving you a second time when you were depending on me. I honestly didn't think there was a way around this problem. Bernie means a great deal to me. He's more than just my boss; he's one of my best friends. I didn't think I could let him down."

Annie placed one finger across his lips. "I know. I understand. As you said the day you left, I wouldn't love you if you were the type of man to leave a friend in the lurch. I know how important this case is to you. I just needed some time to think about my feelings. I finally realized what I was seeking here in Summerly, the comfort and sense of belonging, I also have with you."

"But I let you down again," Tyler pointed out, knowing he could very well be shooting himself in the foot. But he needed to talk this through with Annie before they could possibly think about building a future together.

"You didn't let me down. You made a difficult choice, and I respect that."

"So you forgive me?"

Annie smiled, and Tyler couldn't remember ever

seeing anything so lovely. "There's nothing to forgive."

Hope grew inside him. "Yeah, there probably is, but I appreciate your saying that." He scratched the side of his face. "Because the reason I'm here is to tell you I've come back to Summerly to stay."

"What about your case? What about your boss? I thought he was depending on you?"

Tyler stepped forward and wrapped Annie in a tight embrace again. "He was. But I managed to find another great lawyer to join the firm and take my place. She'll handle the case quite well. And if she needs any help, I'll be available." He grinned. "By phone."

He could see the tears in Annie's eyes as she looked up at him. He only hoped those were tears of joy.

"That's wonderful. But do you really want to move back? I know how much your job at the law firm must mean to you."

"It doesn't mean as much to me as you and Courtney do. Truthfully, I enjoyed working at the store more. There I felt like I was growing a business, adding something to the community. I really liked what I was doing."

"Are you sure? Because I was just packing to go to New York."

Tyler couldn't believe his eyes. For the first time since he'd stepped inside Annie's house, he looked around. Her suitcase was on the floor by the couch.

"Why were you coming to New York?"

She leaned forward and brushed her lips across his. When he tried to deepen the kiss, she backed away. "I was coming to tell you I love you and that I'll marry you and live in New York, if that's what it takes to be with you."

Stunned, Tyler stared at her. "You're kidding, right?"

"Nope. I've been miserable since you left, and eventually, I realized that I wanted to be with you. No matter what. No matter where."

Tyler felt like he'd just won the lottery. He gathered Annie into a tight embrace. "Well, if it's all the same to you, I think I'd like to stay here in Summerly. Now about that getting married part—"

Annie kissed him again. "I'm afraid that's non-negotiable, counselor. It's marriage or nothing. I'm not the sort for an affair."

Tyler chuckled, feeling happier than he'd ever felt. He wasn't sure he deserved to be this happy. But thankfully, he'd found Annie again after all these years.

"My sentiments, exactly," he said, giving her a quick kiss. "I want to get married. And maybe have a couple of children."

"I'd love to have a couple of children too," she said with a smile.

He grinned. "Annie Palmer Wylie, I love you."

"I love you too."

Tyler wrapped Annie in his arms and kissed her, knowing that after all these years, he'd finally found his way back home.